The Sand, The Wind, The Night

Ken Green

Gotham Books

30 N Gould St.
Ste. 20820, Sheridan, WY 82801
https://gothambooksinc.com/

Phone: 1 (307) 464-7800

© 2023 Ken Green. All rights reserved.

No part of this book may be reproduced, stored in a retrieval system, or transmitted by any means without the written permission of the author.

Published by Gotham Books (February 7, 2023)

ISBN: 979-8-88775-051-4 (sc)
ISBN: 979-8-88775-052-1 (e)

Because of the dynamic nature of the Internet, any web addresses or links contained in this book may have changed since publication and may no longer be valid.

The views expressed in this work are solely those of the author and do not necessarily reflect the views of the publisher, and the publisher hereby disclaims any responsibility for them.

The Sand

[1]

The battered Range Rover rocked gently in the violet wind before dawn. Speckles of sand clicked against hollow metal and pitted glass. Clothed heavily in worn army fatigues, Chloe sat shivering in the front passenger seat, a bundle of blond and olive green. Her breath condensed in the dank space before her. An Arab driver coughed, reached into the layers of his clothing and extracted a plain brown packet of cigarettes. He tapped out a single dew-stained cigarette carefully preventing stale tobacco from spilling out the ends and struck fire. Acrid smoke filtered over to Chloe, stinging her eyes. He didn't offer her one. She had already refused twice.

She wiped a patch of condensation from the window with her coat sleeve. Outside, shadows lurked, some moving, others still. She closed her eyes and let her mind drift listening to the flecks of sand. It was a familiar sound, precise and molecular. Incandescent lights appeared from her memory. Matted grass under a blanket crust of frost crinkled beneath her feet. A tarpaulin snapped briskly overhead. It was a carnival of swirling shadows and static electricity, of sugar crystals spinning against aluminum and miraculously evaporating and materializing as wispy pink flax, sticky cotton candy. The present dissipated into a hypnotic ether of sound, of sand, and wind, and night.

A' Salam Alaykum." A greeting from the driver's side of the vehicle startled her. Chloe turned and caught the full glare of an LED flashlight. She blinked and turned as the sharp beam scanned the vacant seats. Apparently satisfied, the light switched back into darkness. Knuckles rapped on the glass. The driver hastily stubbed his cigarette and lowered the window. Cold air hustled in.

[2]

A phone rang insistently in the digital glow of a bedstand clock. Kevin rolled over in a tangle of sheets and bedcovers and disengaged the receiver while reaching for the light. A glass of water thumped onto the rug. "Hello? Yeah. Um?" He sat up and moaned. The quartz heart beat was at 3:08. "Yes, I'm awake. What?"

A female voice, distorted by an incomprehensibly vast web of wires, satellites and switches, slipped into a bureaucratic drawl, distant and mechanically impersonal like elevator music. "Sparrow passed through Rome. Beirut is not her destination. You will now transit at Malta. Air France from Charles de Gaulle leaves 10 A.M. Confirm."

"Got it," Kevin responded, parroting the information. The line went dead. "Bitch," he muttered and flicked off the light. The crimson glow pulsed 3:11.

[3]

Los Angeles International Airport, LAX, was busy as it forever is on Saturday evenings. Vehicles bumped along the lower inner tarmac loop in a despondent crawl. Heavy pedestrian traffic trundled through the terminal's automatic doors. Each time the hydraulics relaxed allowing the glass plates to slide together another hurried foot descended on the rubber floor pads forcing them apart. It was wearying watching them, waiting for them to close, just once.

"There! No, almost." Dean sighed. He tapped his foot and returned his gaze to the crowd. He stood in his personal island of calm holding a sign above his head. FLOWERS was printed in bold letters on plain cardboard.

Two girls stopped and asked the nice Mexican-American gentleman, "How much?"

"Sorry?" he answered impatiently.

"A dozen roses would be nice for mother," one girl said to the other.

"No kidding? Really?" Dean replied with a lecherous smirk. She pointed at his sign with a questioning look. "Go on get out of here," he moaned wearily. The girls shrugged and retreated giggling. Dean glanced at the magazine gift shop he was standing overly close to. Embarrassed, he moved further away, scanning the throng expectantly.

A tall man in his late thirties, well dressed but veiled with sunglasses, snaked purposefully through the arrivals gate. He went directly to Dean. "Flowers has been delayed in New York," he said with a hint of a smirk. "Maybe permanently. I'm Redlinger. Bob Redlinger."

Oh, okay. How ya doing Bob? Welcome to paradise. The name's Dean." He extended his hand for the customary handshake. It didn't come. "Great," Dean mumbled. "You got any bags, sir?" he asked with an emphasis on sir.

Redlinger was carrying only a briefcase. "No. Just this. Let's go," he answered brusquely.

"Yeah, yeah, okay. This way," Dean said.

Dean directed him towards the automated doors, which were now stuck closed. They shoved their way through a manual side door onto the pavement outside and Dean guided towards a discreetly beige colored van sporting an orange "ChemSearch" logo on its side. A cop was eying the vehicle and thumbing his tablet of citations.

"Hey, this is a pick-up zone, right? So, I'm picking up." Dean glared at the officer. "And this is my passenger. So, stick your tickets right in your – "The traffic cop advanced with a dangerous glower. "-pocket," Dean finished sheepishly. The two climbed aboard and Dean eased cautiously into the stream of vehicles.

"You picked a fine time to arrive, you know?" Dean said, picking up a microphone and calling, "Dispatch Zone A. Zone A, this is Dean in unit 5. Code arrived. Negative Flowers, replacement is Redlinger. Repeat. Redlinger."

A voice came back, "Roger 5. Maintain destination. Dispatch clear."

"Right. 5 clear." He replaced the mike. "Man, would you look at this," Dean complained gesturing at the traffic. He glanced in the mirror. Redlinger gazed out the window acknowledging nothing. "Yep, that's really something," he muttered quietly.

The van inched along Century Boulevard, an insect in an insect flow. It crawled onto the freeway and joined the masses creeping cautiously home. By dusk, the traffic had thinned into excited motion and Dean was cruising at a comfortable 65 mph, heading north away from the city. Redlinger was smoking, quiet but attentive. Dean, long given up on conversation, watched the oncoming river turn into a stream of bright fire as headlights flared on. He liked this terrible wonder of Southern California, the transition into night. He toyed with the idea of grabbing and tossing Redlinger's cigarette out the window and found a brief respite from the oppressive silence.

[4]

A dim light bulb, stuttering a pitiful carrot glow, hung in its rusty socket at the end of a tattered wire. A breeze stirred it against the dust crusted telephone pole from which it dangled. It was the last pole and the final light along an outskirt street that disintegrated with its sidewalk into potholes and sand. The street was lined with modest unfinished concrete residences. A well-manicured shop was tucked discreetly in at the far end. Silhouettes of the Great Pyramid tombs themselves loomed in the darkness, vigilant specters of the drift of time. Beyond was plateau and desert.

A brightly painted sign swung over the door proclaiming, Ali Mohamed Mahmoud's Egyptian Souvenirs, in Arabic, French, English and German. The windows were framed with unlit lights and conspicuously clean. They were barred, padlocked, and full of alabaster busts of Nefertiti and the gods of upper and lower Egypt, replicas of the Sphinx and the great pyramid of Cheops, blue lapis beads, elegant pink coral, the key of life shimmering in gold and silver, and myriads more of the essential been-there-done-that souvenir tourist tokens.

A sparrow landed on the wire and ruffled its feathers. The light died. At the sound of an approaching motor, the musty bird took flight into a scarcely graying dawn. A motorcycle approached from town, its single headlight bobbing through the early morning mist. As it grew near, the rider quietened the engine and coasted to a halt in front of the shop. A young Arab in Egyptian Army fatigues jumped off, retrieved a key from under a potted plant by the door and entered. Bells jingled softly overhead, and jangled again as the door closed.

Ahmed picked up a silver donkey from a shelf and laughed quietly. The shop was cluttered as always. He passed through another door and stood listening in the hallway at the end of a staircase. He hung his coat and went into a larger living room, gaudily furnished to Egyptian taste. He lay down on a luxurious couch. "Too early to wake anyone," he murmured and fell quickly asleep.

(5)

Lindsey Merric sat back from the table glancing at a night blackened window and ran his hand wearily through his auburn hair. The warped reflection showed a casually dressed tall middle-aged man, white ruffled shirt, undone tie, collar open. He needed a shave. He turned from the window and reached for a gold pack of English cigarettes. He tapped them absently and gazed at the others in the conference room. They were gazing back. Sheldon Ryders, desk officer for Beirut, red hair, stocky with a bright green tie still in place, Irish. Scott

Freeman, the Cairo man, fair hair, slim, six-foot, sleeves rolled up, blue tie just loose enough for comfort. Gloria Lang-Anker, his secretary for four or five years, pale, streaks of grey in her peppery beige tresses, unmarried, nursing a cold with tissues and cough drops, traces of lines around the eyes. All four were grouped at one end of a long mahogany conference table. The other chairs were empty and the far end of the room was in shadow.

"I apologize and thank you again for sacrificing your Saturday evening for this meeting," Lindsey said somberly. He checked the gold Rolex on his wrist. "It is nearly eleven. We'll summarize and call it a night. Gloria?"

Gloria looked at her notes and cleared her throat. "As far as we know, Sparrow is now in Libya. It is unexpected since all indications were that she was headed routinely back to Beirut. She changed planes in Frankfurt, this time, and headed to Rome, on Thursday. She boarded an Air Malta flight and flew to Luqa airfield. We alerted Malta from Italy so we were able to pick her up again leaving customs on the island. She took a cab to Valletta and went to a photography shop owned by a ..." She turned a page. "...a Mr. Farugia, a native Maltese and someone we are already familiar with. He was linked some years ago with Yemen after the Lebanese civil war. Our Beirut staff stumbled onto his Yemeni-Mediterranean contraband route. A backdoor man, so to speak, into Saudi and the Arabian Peninsula. Some influence in Somalia.

When Israel invaded southern Lebanon in 2006, he moved operations to the Maltese Islands. What Sparrow has to do with him is anyone's guess. We lost her there until Saturday, this morning, when local customs reported her boarding the morning Libyan Jamhuria Airways flight to Tripoli. There she was met and driven into a military controlled section of the airport where we were unable to follow. Her digression to Rome threw our plans for Hawk off, so we held him over in Paris till we knew what Sparrow was doing. He is now rerouted to Malta where we'll keep him for now." She sniffled into a tissue and looked up from her notes.

"Thanks, Gloria," Lindsey said. "Our best guess is that Chloe-Sparrow was flown by a Libyan military plane to one of the many bases in the central Sahara. This is her first deviation from her usual bi-monthly route from Zurich to Frankfurt and then nonstop to Beirut in, well, since December, just over six months. Sheldon?"

Sheldon tapped his pen on the shiny mahogany, toying with it. "Well, we've kept an eye on this girl since we caught on to her travel pattern to Lebanon two years ago. It seemed like a possible lead at the time. She's varied schedule twice since then, once to southern California and once to Paris where she was spotted with some student radicals who were later arrested for a botched attempt to blow up a bridge across the Seine in the Saint-Michel district as some kind of protest." He shrugged.

Lindsey, distracted again by his reflection, said, "Thanks Shel. Scott?"

Scott leaned forward peering over his wire rim bifocals. "As you know, we haven't got much to go on. Wally Kitterman in Cairo uncovered indications of arms and explosives movement between Yemen and Libya through the Suez. Some night workers at Port Said were injured when a crate carrying what should have been VCRs was accidentally dropped. What spilled out were packages of various raw explosives. Work should have stopped then and there but the remaining cargo was loaded onto a Greek freighter before Egyptian authorities from Cairo could get there. By morning, the freighter, the Lydia, had sailed and was reported entering Tripoli harbour two days later. That was last April. These types of shipments are fronted by various import-export firms in Cairo, Istanbul, Athens, Beirut, etc. The transit disguises of choice are light electronics and tourist souvenirs and the like. Our computers linked some of the names in this particular incident with our girl's regular contacts in Beirut. A slim connection, but a connection nonetheless."

Lindsey Merric crumpled a piece of paper and tossed the wad into a corner wastebasket. "Right, thanks, all." He yawned and stretched. "That leaves Sparrow somewhere in Libya and our Hawk on his way to Malta where we'll just have to leave him until his prey resurfaces. We may as well go home and get some rest while we're waiting on this one."

The four rose as one, donning jackets, straightening ties, skirt and blouse, packing papers and snapping briefcases. Lindsey ushered the others into the carpeted hallway. "We should be hearing around noon-ish …" His voice trailed off as the door eased itself shut. The lights automatically dimmed.

- - -

Some minutes later, a janitor in dark blue coveralls pushed the door open. He bypassed the skewed chairs, reached under the mahogany tabletop and passed a compact electronic wand camouflaged as a common ball point pen over a tiny device embedded in the wood. He clicked the pen once transferring the information from the micro-recorder to the pen. He briefly checked a meter carefully incorporated into the pocket clasp of the pen, then immediately clicked it again, twice, to clear the data from and to reset the recorder. He checked the readings again and got a neutral signal from under the table followed by a tiny light blip that confirmed it was working. He twisted the ink cartridge end a full double turn and the pen disconnected from any electronic signature it might emit. He made a note with the pen on his janitorial check list, another room cleaned for the night.

He straightened the chairs, wiped the table surface with a clean rag and left. The reflections on the windows died as the lights slowly dimmed unveiling a black tree line accented with moonlight.

(6)

"Alaykum A' Salam," the driver answered. He leaned out and shook a calloused hand of the heavily armed soldier with the flashlight. Chloe peered over but it was too dark to see clearly. She heard guttural Arabic and a name, Al Sebha. The soldier withdrew into the gloom shouting orders into the deeper darkness. Motors coughed into life and forms flickered in the sudden bright headlights. Silhouetted in the glaring illumination, Chloe felt helpless and exposed.

A string of airfield lights flared on as the twin engines of an ancient DC3 fired, revved, and churned up swirls of sand against the Range Rover. The soldiers and the trucks all but disappeared momentarily under a gritty cloud. With a muffled drone the plane vanished down the desert track and lifted into the approaching dawn.

"We are to follow the trucks," the driver announced apologetically. Chloe nodded as the Rover stirred and fell jerkily in behind two army trucks already in motion. The small caravan jostled and bumped away from the tinted horizon into the vast and all but trackless Sahara. A solitary Libyan soldier watched them go.

When the column had faded, he turned to his vehicle, switched off the landing field lights and hauled them in like an oversized string of Christmas bulbs. He disconnected them from the battery power source and heaved them into a large wooden box in the rear. Uncovering a compact transmitter, he plugged in earphones, tapped the appropriate keys and spoke a brief message in Arabic. The answer came back and he signed off. Before shutting down, he rapidly punched in another number and urgently repeated a jumble of letters and numbers, covering his voice with a heavy French accent.

In a trailer, tens of horizons distant, a technician was reading, relaxed on a comfortable camp bed. One end of the trailer was packed with electronic equipment, oilfield monitors and a computer terminal. Music played softly. A red light blinked on and a buzzer sounded. The technician leapt to his feet and bounded towards the computer. It was a standard rig monitoring setup but with a special coding modification that was known only to this one man in the field. A brief message materialized on a data print out. He deciphered the note quickly and immediately punched out an answering code on the keyboard.

The soldier listened intently to the string of sounds in his earphones. Relieved, he switched off his set, secured it in its pouch and clambered into his disheveled SUV. The sun was breaking over the distant dunes. There was a long drive ahead.

[7]

Kevin leaned forward in a grand armchair and finished tying his shoes. His shirt was unbuttoned and hung loose. With one hand he clutched a fresh white towel and tousled his damp hair. The other hand reached for the phone and punched a single digit for room service. This was a small hotel near the Charles de Gaul airport. The morning was unusually bright and fresh. Kevin had opened the windows and curtains wide to honor the occasion. The view showed roof tops and distant white monuments. Montmartre, he thought, and a glimpse of the needle of the Eiffel Tower. He preferred to stay further in town, but this wasn't a pleasure call, he reminded himself.

A voice answered on the line. "Bon matin. Je veux un café au lait sans sucre, deux ouefs et jambon, jus d'orange, et un journal en Anglais, s'il vous plait," Kevin requested. A brief pause was filled with a question. "What? Quoi? Non, boiled dans eau chaud. Je ne sais pas le mot … Oui, c'est juste. Oui, merci." He hung the phone up and disappeared into the bathroom. Ten minutes later, he reappeared, clean shaven, shirt tucked in, tie in place. He whistled and walked over to the dresser where his slim briefcase lay open by his jacket. In a neat pile in the case were his diplomatic passport, credit cards, various papers and a compact revolver in a shoulder holster. On the floor was the only other luggage he traveled with, a neatly packed carry-on, ready to go.

He picked up the holster, removed the automatic pistol and walked over to the window. He examined the firearm in the streaming sunlight. The solid weight of a full ammunition clip gave him a sense of reassurance. He looked into the distance and shrugged, "Paris. I should have been in Beirut yesterday, and now I'm going to Malta."

A sharp rapping sounded at the door followed by a waiter's nervous voice calling, "Monsieur? Votre petit-dejeuner."

Kevin held the revolver out of sight behind his back and answered, "Oui, entrez. La porte est ouvert." The rapping repeated. Kevin answered louder with some impatience, "Oui, entrez! Come in, s'il vous bloody plait!"

With sudden ferocity, the door was flung open and the waiter, shoved from behind, stumbled in off balance. The breakfast tray scattered before the falling man. Kevin caught a glimpse of a silver tray and coffee pot suspended in midair, flying bread rolls, dishes, jam and butter, followed by a more sinister vision of a man in black coming through the doorway gun in hand, spurting soundless death. Black hood, black turtleneck, black pants, black sneakers. The unearthly scene unfolded in eerie slow motion in a halo of destruction.

The waiter caught the first blind volley and was flung onto the carpet badly wounded. A steady arc of bullets curved towards its primary target. A dull shuddering cut across the windows disintegrating them in a crescendo of shattering glass and shredding curtains. Kevin had automatically dropped behind an armchair at the first scent of trouble and flicked off the safety latch on his weapon. As fluffs of upholstery ripped away above his head, he stood, raised his revolver and professionally fired two rapid double volleys, one, two, pause, one, two.

With no muffler, the gun roared in the confined space and echoed painfully off the walls. The intruder recoiled against the door from the force of two hits, both Teflon coated. The would-be assassin spun and fell into the hallway, his gun clattering to a halt in the ruins of the breakfast tray where the waiter lay unconscious in a growing pool of blood. An abrupt silence rang in Kevin's head. He shoved his gun into his briefcase, slammed it shut, grabbed his travel bag and plunged into the hallway making for the nearest service exit. Angry and frightened voices echoed in the corridor.

Pausing between flights on the concrete stairwell, Kevin slipped into his jacket and checked for tell tale signs of a struggle. There were none. He took deep breaths to calm his racing heart, walked slowly down the last stairs and stepped gingerly into the bedlam of the lobby. He strode over to the registration counter with a questioning look and glanced over his shoulder at the commotion. The hotel staff was attempting to regain order over hysterical guests and curious onlookers filing in from the street.

"Qu'es-que c'est? What is happening?" he shouted with confused concern in his voice. The receptionist girl barely heard him. He slipped unnoticed out the front doors and into the first cab at the corner. The wail of police and ambulance sirens was closing in. Kevin leaned towards the front seat so he could straighten his tie in the mirror. "L'aeroporte La Bourget," he told the driver. As they rounded the block and passed the hotel, the driver pointed at the police cars. "Je ne sais pas," Kevin shrugged. "C'est toujours la meme chose, tourists, bloody tourists."

"Ah oui," the driver answered and launched into a philosophical discussion about visitors to Paris, immigrants, the government and the global weather. It kept him occupied most of the way to the airport. "Vous etes Anglais?"

"D'accord," Kevin lied. No point in anyone remembering an American.

(8)

The morning sun shone a brilliant silken sheen through the lace curtains in the dining room of Ahmad's father. A glass chandelier above the table twinkled with all the colours of the rainbow. Seated around an elaborately laid breakfast were Ahmed, the young Egyptian soldier on leave, his younger brother Khalid, his baby sister, and mother and father. This was the family and habitat of Ali Muhammad Mahmoud. This is what the Egyptian Souvenir Shop of Giza nourished and gave life. Ahmed was happy to be there.

His father leaned over and poured himself another cup of thick black coffee. "And what are your plans now, Ahmed?" he asked his son.

"I have two weeks all to myself, and of course Fatima. We are going to her parents' beach house west of Iskanderia. We have tickets for the train on Tuesday."

"That sounds nice, but I was hoping you might do me a favour," his father replied.

"Oh, oh. I know you, Father. That sounds like work," Ahmed responded cautiously.

"Well, in a way it is," his father confessed.

"I only have two weeks," Ahmed complained with a thinly concealed whine.

"Ahmed!" his mother scolded to the chorus of snickers from his siblings. The young soldier opened his mouth to protest but his father held up his hand.

"How would you and Fatima like to spend a week in Athens? All expenses paid, of course."

Ahmed brightened. "Athens?" he asked suspiciously.

Ali Mahmoud chuckled. "I have a special large shipment of Indian medallions, native Balucchi, very rare that are arriving from Yemen where they were smuggled to. Nothing really illegal. It is mostly to avoid unreasonable custom duties." He winked. "But it is delicate enough to require personal attention. I want you to see them put safely on a ship to America at the Athenian port of Piraeus."

With the matter settled, the head of the household rose from the table and led his small tribe to the veranda. The Great Pyramids shimmered in the near distance. "Even after fifty-eight years, I never tire of this sight," he sighed. It was the one thing the family always agreed on.

[9]

The ChemSearch van snaked its way up a twisting dirt road into the night shrouded foothills east of Ventura. The headlights slashed back and forth with the turns, cutting into the roadside brush then shining out over dark gully voids. Crickets screeched incessantly in the dusty bushes just audible over the road noises. Dean prodded the light button on his digital wristwatch. "Just about nine o'clock," he announced proudly. "We made pretty good time." He didn't expect a response and none came.

The van turned onto a short tarmac stretch and stopped at a wrought iron gate. Dean leaned out and waved a plastic card across a security eye. The gates swung open with barely a creak. Dean eased the van through and continued a few hundred yards up a thickly paved driveway to the brightly lit façade of a medium sized mansion.

A casually well-dressed man opened the heavy front door and came onto the terrace as the van coasted to a halt. He was tall and moderately handsome. He was accompanied by a striking young woman with dark hair, amber eyes and a velvet smile, his secretary, companion and lover. Dean climbed from behind the wheel. "Hello, Mr. Bellard. Hi, Julia. Beautiful evening, eh?"

Hank Bellard was one of those ex-oilmen of which the retired world seems so full. He looked sturdy and uncompromising, as should be expected of a man who had for much of his life wrestled oilfield equipment around the globe and dealt directly with governments, kings and dictators. A tint of red in his hair and moustache gave him an independent flair. It also left one with the feeling that somewhere not far below the surface a fire was smoldering. He was a Texan, or more appropriately had been one. These days he was "difficult to place", a shade beyond geographical ties.

"That's right, Dean, California nights," Hank answered. "How's the wife?"

"Better, thanks. No Covid, thank you, just this damn flu," Dean replied. Redlinger came around the van, briefcase in hand. Dean made the introductions. "Bob Redlinger, Hank Bellard."

"Hello, Bob," Hank greeted the man, heartily shaking hands before Redlinger had a chance to avoid him. "Welcome to California. It beats New York this time of year even with our smog. Call me Hank and this is Julia, my secretary."

"Hello," Redlinger responded shortly. There was an awkward pause.

Hank coughed into his fist. "Yes, well, let's go inside. Dean, will you bring Redlinger's bag in?"

"This is it," Redlinger said, holding up his case. "I won't be here long. Mr. Xenox has a jet coming to Ventura for me at six in the morning. I'll be meeting him in Beijing."

"Right. How is your schedule, Dean? Can you wait around for this?" Hank asked.

"Sorry, Mr. Bellard. Dispatch has me back meeting a cargo flight at LAX at eight."

"Okay, I'll run him down myself. Give my best to Katie and the kids."

"Thanks, Mr. Bellard. Goodnight, Julia." Dean aimed the van out the driveway and was swallowed by the night before Hank closed the door behind Julia, himself and his guest.

(10)

Twenty minutes later, somewhat far from the main highway, the ChemSearch van rolled into the first service station Dean saw with public telephones. Cell reception in these hills was notoriously unreliable. An attendant came out wiping his hands with a greasy rag. "Unleaded," Dean called. "Full, okay? And write me out a receipt, would you? Thanks, kid." Not too many of these mom-and-pop places left, he thought striding to the nearest phone bubble. He deposited coins and tapped out a number.

"Hello. Yeah, Dean here. Uh, huh. Flowers didn't show. He was replaced by someone named Bob Redlinger. Uh, huh. Redlinger. A real New York asshole. I don't know where they keep getting them from. Look, he's flying out by private jet in the morning at six. From up here, going to Beijing to meet X. I think we need to let our Chinese friends know we want to keep an eye on them. Yep, okay, thanks. How're the wife and kids?" A string of noises came through the line. "I know you're not married." Dean held the receiver slightly away from his ear. "Have a nice evening," he said with a smirk and hung up. He paid the attendant with cash, took his receipt and drove onto the road. Recognizing a murmur on the radio, he turned the volume up and listened to the end of "Ventura Highway" before turning it down again.

(11)

The living room at Hank Bellard's place would have made Frank Lloyd Wright, if not envious, at least proud that someone had taken his clues to heart and built around them. The rough brick fireplace commanded the central living space towards which plush earth tone armchairs and an elaborately functional leather couch were directed. A wide screen television was tucked discreetly into a bookshelf on the room's periphery. Logs were carefully stacked behind an iron grate but were not lit nor would they be for several months.

Julia excused herself for the night. "See you in the morning, Hank. Nice meeting you, Mr. Redlinger. Goodnight." Bellard watched admiringly as she glided through the doorway. He counted himself a lucky man.

"What'll it be? Scotch? Bourbon?" he asked from a corner bar.

"Plain Scotch on ice will be fine," Redlinger answered.

Hank poured two while picking up the topic which brought the two men together. "So, Mr. Xenox is in Beijing?" He handed the other man his drink.

"Yes. Production has already begun. He wanted me to make a final design compatibility check at Zhangjiang." Redlinger opened his briefcase and unfolded a thin stack of blueprints onto a low redwood coffee table. "Here, nothing very difficult."

Outside, the moon rose from behind the surrounding hills. A lanky condor swooped through the cool air and landed, clawing at a sturdy branch. It furled its long floppy wings in a clumsy ballet of balance and settled into the security of its native vegetation. The great vulture craned its neck and surveyed its silvery domain. Crickets whined to a shrill climax, and then fell steadily into silence, before restarting the night long cycle of noise and quiet over again, and again, and again until dawn.

[12]

The desert stretched blindly out in all directions. What should have been horizon dissolved into shimmering heat ripples. Sand floated in pools of reflected sky. The interior of the Range Rover was cool. It was an officer's vehicle and properly air conditioned. The convenience was out of consideration for the blond Western woman who rode next to the Libyan driver. Chloe had removed the olive jacket in which she had been bundled during the cool night and was now sweating lightly in a thin utility shirt, slacks and desert boots. She gazed from behind dark sunglasses at an obscurity that was difficult to comprehend.

"Our destination?" she asked. It was the first she had spoken in hours.

The driver answered simply, "Oasis." The wheels sung over the hot sand.

"How far?" she prodded.

"Not far. Soon. Important people." The driver had been instructed to tell little, only what was necessary. It was a task that came naturally to his desert people. Saharan survival depended historically on protected tribal secrets, and this girl was just a foreigner. A half hour later, he nudged Chloe from her thoughts and pointed.

Ahead and taking form from within the liquid heat waves, Chloe could just distinguish the shapes of the two army trucks they had started to travel with but had long since separated from. They were pulled up around a group of tents and several unfinished low concrete buildings. A small herd of camels became visible along with a flock of scraggly goats. "Bedu well, water," the driver offered as explanation. "Army houses."

The vehicle strained to a halt in a cloud of dust amidst a pandemonium of voices. The driver labored out, stiff from the cramped drive and shouting along with the rest. Chloe veiled her thoughts and avoided looking at the cluster of Bedu children gathered around her window. One boy with a fly along the rim of one eye pointed a revolver at her and pulled the trigger. The hammer clicked sickeningly and the child laughed maliciously. Chloe shuddered. She flashed back to when a young, arrogant Israeli soldier had given her a cruel prodding with a machine gun muzzle at a West Bank checkpoint once long ago. A Libyan soldier descended, cursing, and the urchins scattered.

With more commotion, banging and shouting, soldiers brought tin jerry cans from one of the concrete buildings and refueled the Range Rover. Another group unloaded some boxes, barrels and sacks from the trucks and carried them to the outpost's veranda. These tasks completed, they climbed back onboard. The two trucks disappeared into the desert behind a flurry of dust and pebbles. Chloe's driver came from the building and approached her window. She lowered it.

"We wait here, one maybe two days. People not yet at oasis," he announced. Chloe's face revealed nothing, her face remained expressionless. "There is a room for you," the driver added nervously.

[13]

Kevin sat with an iced lime vodka tonic on a glass table next to him toying with a high-powered pair of binoculars. He gazed at the blue Mediterranean three floors down and less than a hundred feet away. A cluster of brightly coloured fishing boats tugged at their anchor lines in the afternoon swell. A sail surfer knifed colourfully across the bay. A group of scuba divers were suiting up for an excursion. Kevin watched as they boarded a flat bottom boat and headed out to deeper water. In the room, a Maltese man was drinking a coffee and reading purposelessly through a hotel complimentary magazine. He was overweight and sloppy in the traditional Mediterranean way. Kevin called to him.

"David. I could use a little relaxation. Think you could fix me up for an hour or two of scuba diving this evening?" David, in loose trousers, a T-shirt and sneakers, padded out onto the balcony and leaned on the railing. He was the Maltese do-all man who worked at the American consulate in Floriana.

"Yeah, sure. I know the owner." He pointed to the skiff. "A good friend of my family. My cousin works there. The Blue Grotto is a good place on the other side of the island. The water is clear. You want a guide? Or you prefer to dive alone?"

"Depends on who the guide is," Kevin responded. David followed the binoculars' line of vision.

"That's Silvia, my cousin. She's the guide."

Kevin watched as the boat disappeared behind an outcropping of gnarly limestone rocks. "Then I would be a fool to go alone."

(14)

The Egypt Air 737 roared its engines and rumbled down the runway, climbing into the air and simultaneously turning in an expansive circle to gain altitude. It tipped its wings over the Pyramids of Giza, skirting above the borderland between endless desert waste and the emerald strip that is the Nile River and cradle of Western civilization. It headed across the expanse of the delta that flowered out towards the hazy Mediterranean Sea.

The seat belt lights winked out with an accompanying dong from the speakers. A stewardess came down the isle offering colas in plastic cups. Ahmed took one and passed another to the girl beside him. "Athens," he laughed. Fatima giggled. "Six more months of that miserable army and we will be free to get married," Ahmed stated matter-of-factly. "And with father's business doing so well, we should be able to take trips like this every year," he added as an afterthought.

He fiddled with the ticket folder and found the itinerary. "We have reservations at the Grand Hellenic and Mr. Papenicholeu, father's Greek agent, will meet us the day after tomorrow to take us to the shipping warehouses at Piraeus."

Fatima was pensive but happy. "Can we go to the Acropolis?" she asked. Twenty-six thousand feet below, the shadow of the aging jetliner raced across the

North African coastline and onto the water where it would languor for the next few hours before coming to rest on the rich soil of Greece.

(15)

The Mediterranean, when caught at the right time and place, is as beautiful as any sea on Earth. This afternoon it appeared to have reached a zenith of glory. Its ultramarine surface was calm and sparkled in the sun. Scarcely a ripple stirred against the grey hull of the colossal warship. The USS Endeavor, aircraft carrier and flagship of the Mediterranean Sixth Fleet, lay becalmed, lazing with the tides, tethered to the sea floor with a single massive anchor. Beyond the northwestern horizon lay the southern tip of Italy. The northeastern horizon concealed the Greek Peloponnesian Peninsula. An F/A 18 Hornet fighter jet growled on deck and catapulted in a trail of high octane fumes off into maneuvers.

The admiral's quarters were elegantly simple, soothingly painted in the light military green intended to maintain a sane disposition even under the most stressful of conditions. A heavy brass porthole provided a clear view of the water and allowed the sun's reflection to play across the ceiling and walls. The commanding officer of the United States presence in the Mediterranean Sea was seated at his desk, leaning back and studying the crisscrossing patterns of sunlight. The cabin was cool and comfortable, the door secured customarily wide open.

An aide entered from the corridor. "Sir, this just came in from Tripoli," he announced handing over an electronic card.

"Thanks, Tim," the admiral answered informally. "Would you bring up some fresh coffee?"

"Yes sir," the aide answered, exiting. The admiral studied the message card for a moment, then selected a brass key from his pocket chain, opened a locked drawer and removed a cipher decoding terminal similar to a credit card machine. He inserted the card and waited for the message to appear on the main desk screen.

The aide returned with a thermos, clean cups and a plate of biscuits on a tray, placed it on a stand and removed the tray that was there. The admiral grunted acknowledgement without looking up. The aide waited quietly. He knew better than to disturb the "old guy" when he was preoccupied.

The screen typed out a cryptic message: "Sparrow enroute to Sebha Oasis." The admiral scribbled a reply to Tripoli, added his and the ship's identification codes and removed the card and handed it and the note to his aide.

"Tim, let Tripoli know we've received them and relay this on to Langley, priority one."

"Yes. Sir," Tim responded and hurried off. Another jet roared on deck causing the sunlight to flutter. The admiral looked pensively at a photo of his family and sighed. He opened a real estate brochure from Scottsdale, Arizona and thumbed through it.

(16)

A row of violet airfield lights glowed in the dew. It was morning, but not yet dawn. A Gulfstream IV class jet had just landed and taxied to a delicate pause on the damp tarmac. Its engines idled with piercing shrillness as it waited for two men at the base steps to finish their shouting. Through the telephoto lens, Redlinger and Bellard seemed like over animated puppets characterizing life, without life's inconveniences. Click. Click. It was classic marionette theatre. Click. The ritual ended. One man climbed the short stairway and ducked into the plane. The other slipped into a dark SUV and drove towards an exit gate.

The plane lurched forward, increased its pace and hurled itself in Dean's direction. He lowered the Nikon and held his ears as twin jets lacerated the sky above him. He watched the jet disappear into low lying clouds in the direction of the Pacific. He listened until its growl faded, then returned to his van. He removed the camera's digital card, plugged it into a laptop. He checked the airport's Wi-Fi signal and tapped the send key. Humming softly, he headed the vehicle towards L.A.

"Ca-California, so many good things to see. Ca-California, so many people to be." That was all he could recall, so he sang the lines three times before remembering an Englishman had written them, and stopped.

(17)

A vintage 60's Mercedes bumped along a roughly paved road that coursed through the Maltese countryside between stone walls, barbed wire fences and oil drum barriers. Villages rattled by, each looking about the same as the last, and the next. Identical limestone houses, apartment blocks, and dome capped churches were echoed across the island creating an illusion of traveling through a single extended town. It takes a diligent eye to distinguish and appreciate the many subtle aesthetic differences of the country.

Kevin wasn't feeling particularly diligent as the car skirted some low cliffs and dropped along a twisting valley path to sea level. David was driving. "We've some magnificent rock formations and cliffs on this side of the island. And blue sea like you've never seen. I guarantee it personally," he said.

Kevin grunted acknowledgement and asked "your cousin will be there?"

"Sylvia? Sure. She'll have all the gear. Wet suit, weights, mask, flippers, air tanks. The works. Enjoy yourself." David beamed.

Kevin winked. "I'll do my best." Both laughed.

The car wound through a series of sharp bends and descended into a small settlement where the road abruptly ended at a shop-café parking lot. Everything was closed and no one was about. Several brightly painted fishing boats were beached in a tidy row along a concrete ramp that led into the water. A red Alfa Romeo sports convertible was carefully parked near the ramp with diving equipment strewn about. A girl was suiting up as the Mercedes coasted to a halt.

"Hey David," Sylvia called. The Maltese clambered out and embraced his pretty cousin.

"Sylvia, this is Mr. Kevin Varyte." He struggled with the last name briefly. "He is here on holiday from the American embassy in London."

Sylvia shook his hand. "I hope you enjoy your stay. Malta has a way of helping people forget their problems for awhile." They walked towards the pile of gear.

"I always try to leave my worries behind in such beautiful surroundings. And company," Kevin added with a somewhat lascivious grin.

The girl smiled with a hint of a blush. "Hey, David," she called. "Give us a hand here."

Kevin wriggled into his wetsuit and strapped on an oxygen tank and weight belt. It was hot work even in the late afternoon. "You will cool off in the water," Sylvia encouraged. She waved to her cousin. "We'll be back in an hour or so."

"Right you are. I'll be waiting," he responded. Kevin and Sylvia strode awkwardly down the ramp and slid into the cool water. They were quickly engulfed by foaming bubbles. The water was luxuriously refreshing and tingled as it seeped between skin and the insulating wetsuit rubber. Sylvia, distorted and faceless behind her mask, signaled Kevin to follow. He eagerly obeyed.

David lounged by the Mercedes and watched the bubbles until they disappeared some hundred meters further on into the rocks where the Blue Grotto caves lay hidden below the waterline. Kevin kicked his flippers and glided along as the girl led him under arches and through tight passageways that opened up into spacious chambers. Sunlight filtered from above forming glittering curtains against dark shadows and glistening the multicolored corals and fish. Sylvia motioned Kevin to surface. They rose into a cave. The only light shone silvery from the water below an entrance that periodically opened to air with the tides. They climbed onto a tiny beach, giggling.

"One of my favorite spots," Sylvia whispered.

"I can see why," Kevin answered pulling her close. She offered no resistance.

- - -

David stood back and admired his polished automobile. He tossed the wax and rag into the trunk and lit a well-earned cigarette. He started a combination yawn and stretch which he never finished. A muffled rifle cracked through the basking silence from the hillside above. David whirled sideways astonished at the blood welling up around his shoulder. A second shot exploded painfully in his side, jerking him across the hood of the car. He slid gasping in a lubricating trail of blood to the ground as darkness momentarily overwhelmed him. A dim consciousness slowly returned. Flies were irritating his wounds. He struggled to regain control and crawled towards the shelter of the fishing boats where he passed out again.

- - -

Twenty minutes later, Kevin and Sylvia rose laughing from the water and flopped up the boat ramp. Sylvia was first to see David's huddled form and the crimson staining him. "Oh my God! David!" she choked.

Kevin pulled her down between two boats. "Stay down! Whoever did this is probably still around." He could see the movement of David's laborious breathing.

"He's alive," he whispered. They rapidly shed their diving gear. "Where are your keys?" Kevin demanded. Sylvia fumbled with the chain around her neck and handed them shakily to him.

"Stay here," Kevin firmly ordered and ran crouching to David who waved him away.

"I'll be alright. Get Sylvia out of here," he pleaded urgently. "If they wanted me, I'd be dead by now."

Kevin scurried to the Mercedes keeping low, opened the front door and grabbed his jacket and the automatic he always carried with it. A rifle shot thudded into the car but Kevin was well protected from the line of sight. Another followed. Kevin grimaced and sprinted towards the Alpha Romero. Bullets ricocheted in the dust but none found their mark. Kevin ducked into the driver's seat, crouching below the steering wheel, cranked the engine on and revved the gas pedal with his hand. He swung the passenger door open and called to Sylvia, "Now! Quickly! And keep low!"

(18)

Lindsey Merric, Scott Freeman, Sheldon Rynders and Gloria Lang-Anker were gathered again at the Langley headquarters conference room. He held the message that had been relayed by the commander of the USS Endeavor. "Okay, we finally know where Sparrow is leading us. Sebha Oasis. The heart of Colonel Muammar Gaddafi's 1969 Jamahiriya Green Revolution," Lindsey announced. "The Libyans certainly have a flair for dramatics, though what it has to do with today is anyone's guess. In any case, it is reportedly a haven of stability since the Arab Spring Revolution created such instability everywhere else."

"Is Sparrow taking us to her nest?" Sheldon wondered out loud.

"Let's hope so," affirmed Lindsey. "Unfortunately, someone appears to be aware of our surveillance. Paris reports a bit of a shoot up at Kevin's hotel. A room service waiter was badly injured and an unidentified assassin was terminated, a middle easterner. Turkish, Lebanese, Moroccan. Who knows? Could be anything. Left a Russian automatic assault pistol with silencer. All a bit messy. And embarrassing. Kevin was registered as an American businessman, so the gendarmes turned up yelling at our embassy. The question now is do we send him into Libya, or let him sit in Malta where he is in no danger?"

- - -

Sylvia wiped the tears from her cheeks and dove into the car, hunching on the floor. The rifle fired again, this time ripping a neat hole through the windscreen and tearing into the seat inches from Kevin's head. Slamming the car in gear, Kevin punched full throttle in a squealing circle and raced up the hill leaving a trail of smoke and burnt rubber. More shots went wild as the convertible sped up the winding slope away from the sea. From a side road, two men ran out from behind a stone shepherd's shelter splotched with crudely painted political slogans. They ran to a black sedan. Dust swirled as they hurriedly turned to intercept the approaching sports car, but they were too late.

The red convertible swept past the Y intersection a good forty seconds before the black car arrived at the same spot. A small head start, but the Alpha Romero was faster, maneuvered more efficiently, and Kevin was the better driver by far. But where could they go? On a relatively small island one would be unable to evade a determined search for long.

Sylvia directed Kevin inland towards higher ground. They passed down a long tree lined avenue and aimed for a summit town, an ancient fortified city. "Medina," Sylvia shouted. "The Silent City. No cars are allowed inside the walls. We might be able to hide there."

"Or at least fight on even terms," Kevin added cradling his automatic.

- - -

Scott picked nonchalantly at his fingernails. "No point in keeping him idle in Malta," he said.

- - -

The car ripped up the final hill, fishtailed dangerously around a corner and sped through the gates of the Silent City. Annoyed faces from closing shops and sidewalk cafes turned towards the piercing sound of the straining engine. Kevin slid the car to a halt at a metal barrier and bounded out the door with Sylvia in tow. They ran across a short stone bridge spanning a dry moat and entered the castle city. They raced blindly down narrow alleys and emerged onto a spacious cobblestone cathedral square.

Unnoticed in their commotion, dusk had already enveloped them. The last streaks of crimson sun were dying across the sky and a deep azure was blanketing the island in darkness. Sight was growing difficult. They clung to the shadow of the looming cathedral and rapidly worked their way towards the outer city walls which commanded a clear view to the sea miles away. These walls are some of the highest points on the entire island of Malta and stand over a hundred vertical feet above the rocky fields below.

Along the walls at one end of the square, a café lay deserted with empty tables and chairs neatly arranged for the morrow. Residential windows that opened onto the plaza were mostly shuttered, doors mostly closed. The cracks between them were all alive with electric lights. The occupants were sitting for dinner, temporarily ignoring the evening outside.

The slick sound of footsteps echoed from the hollows around the square. The two pursuers appeared nearly simultaneously at opposite ends of the open expanse and halted. One carried what appeared to be a hunting rifle, the weapon from the cove. The other carried a pistol. They peered into the murky shadows but could distinguish very little. They signaled each other and began a cautious sweep in the direction of the outer wall.

- - -

Scott looked up from his fingernails. "I say send him in."

- - -

With a creeping sense of horror at the men's approach, Kevin and the girl ducked amongst the empty tables along the edge of the fortress walls. He signaled her to stay down and with weapon in hand, crept in the direction from which the man with the pistol approached. The man with the rifle searched the far end of the perimeter wall and disappeared momentarily behind a corner of the cathedral. That one was less of a danger at close range, in any case.

- - -

"Fine," Lindsey replied, catching a glimpse of his image in the window. "What do you think, Shel?"

- - -

An imperceptible rustle from a cluster of potted plants cloaked in shadow alerted the Maltese thug. He leveled his pistol but was too late. The butt of Kevin's automatic struck squarely on his temple with muffled force. He sagged forward gun still in hand. Kevin lowered the body, twisted the limp head and gave a sharp jerk, snapping the neck with a sickening crackle. His training was instinctive.

- - -

Sheldon flicked his Ronson lighter on and off, but reached for a pack of Icelandic Xylitol chewing gum instead of his customary Camel. "This quitting smoking is gonna kill me," he commented. "I agree with Scott. We can't leave him in Malta doing nothing."

- - -

The man with the hunting rifle whispered into the darkness, "Joss!" There was no reply. He eased along the outer wall towards the vacant tables where Sylvia crouched. Kevin followed his dim silhouette approaching cautiously. The gangster saw the girl and brought the rifle down to bear on her. "Alright, you. Up slowly," he hissed. Kevin maneuvered behind the man and closed on him carefully. Sylvia stood taking pains not to glance in Kevin's direction. "You're a cute one alright," the man gloated. "Where's your boyfriend?"

"Right behind you, Kevin said, aiming his weapon at the man's back. The man's astonishingly rapid reaction stunned Kevin who unexpectedly felt an agonizing pain in his right hand as the rifle barrel swung around. He watched his automatic clatter onto the paving stones.

- - -

"Send him in," Sheldon said firmly casting his vote.

- - -

The burly Maltese lunged. The force of the attack dragged both men backwards. The neat row of empty tables and chairs scattered noisily in the tussle. The man swung his rifle which Kevin dodged repeatedly. At the first opening, he hurled himself headlong against the man's solid torso and the two staggered back along the low rampart wall. Kevin struggled to regain his balance as the man clawed at his torn shirt. A sharp down thrust of the rifle barrel caught Kevin's upper arm painfully, weakening his defenses just enough to allow the heavy butt to cleave into his ribs on the upswing. The next blow struck his chest, knocking him breathless, but a well-placed forearm deflected the jab at his skull. It crushed into his shoulder instead. Each blow was excruciatingly firm and accurate. Kevin felt his strength ebbing.

He stumbled against the body of the other Maltese and fell. There was one last chance. He clutched the pistol and wrenched it from the inert hand. As he turned to fire, his damaged hand curled in pain and his grip released involuntarily. Panic seared through his veins as he saw the pistol land atop the thick rampart wall and slid the three feet towards the abyss. Kevin lunged after it in a desperate sprawl. His foe was easily ahead of him. He sprung onto the wall and with an evil smirk, kicked the handgun the final inch into space.

Kevin rose up on his knees as to block the next assault. The man swung the heavy rifle forcefully to finish his victim off. A full impact would have easily sent Kevin writhing into empty air, but at the last moment he slithered onto his belly and the blow slipped over his head. The unchecked momentum twisted the attacker precariously off balance and carried him to the edge of the precipice. Kevin kicked out furiously with both feet. The man staggered, momentarily suspended in time as a distorted expression of disbelief turned to one of terror. He dropped with a shivering scream that ended seconds later in an abrupt muffled thud. The rifle collided with the rocks, recoiled and fired.

- - -

Lindsey Merric surveyed the others thoughtfully. "Well, then, it's decided." He turned to his secretary, "Gloria, tell London to 'untether the hawk'."

- - -

Window shutters began to open questioningly onto the square, flooding the darkness with light. Complaining figures appeared at doorways casting shadows on the cobblestones. Kevin and Sylvia withdrew quietly from the Silent City that had, for at least one night, uttered some very disturbing sounds.

(19)

Xandrieu Xenox was a sturdy, olive skinned Greek whose parents had migrated to New York City from a poverty-stricken village on the outskirts of the northeastern city of Thessalonica. His family had spent years manufacturing mud bricks in the ancient fashion, mixing the local red clay with sand and lime, pressing out rows of bricks with wooden blocks, and baking them to a fine hard consistency with wood fires in long iron door kilns. Lengthy days were spent toiling in the smoky odorous yards and unhealthy furnaces. Days grew longer as profits dwindled from the relentless creep of rising costs, slacking sales, imports of more efficient materials and modernization. Even a fair break-even point became difficult to achieve. Eventually, the family reluctantly sat down with a handful of faithful workers and announced the closing of the factory. Concrete and steel were making their business obsolete. The market for bricks was limited and would no longer sustain them. They were through.

The factory was sold to others more willing to take on the new market dynamics. The Xenox family sailed for a fresh start in post-WWII America. Xandrieu, the youngest of six siblings, was merely a baby in his mother's arms when they arrived with the crowds at Ellis Island. Thereafter, it was an uphill run for the boy. Pushed into the wings by his energetic brothers and sisters, and somewhat overlooked by his harried parents, he struggled through an inferior schooling, and struck out in his own solitary directions in the City's tough worlds of intrigue and challenge. His exasperated mother called him aimless, a wanderer, and an unfocused dreamer. His father was less kind and believed his son would end up little more than a bum or a petty criminal.

But Xandrieu was tenacious. He fought the odds without fully understanding them. He clung to his successes, struggled to overcome his failures, and learned the value of friends as well as the threat of enemies. He focused locally and accepted his boundary limits. He drifted towards the docks where he frequently accepted casual labor offers, taking whatever jobs were available at the time, and hung around the bars even more. Gradually, he became aware of the concept of power and learned how to obtain and use it to gain more. By mid-life he found himself in control of his own little niche of the great world in a city he could call his own.

His business was export-import, the life blood of the city, the country and the world. He had carved out his portion of this world and held it well. All was not always legal or fair, and he was the first to admit to this, but it was something that was easily swept under the carpet. As he was fond of saying to his associates, he oft repeated to himself, "It's a fine line, my friends, such a fine line."

- - -

Xenox separated from his contemplation of Beijing's thick smog and fascinating skyline when a well-dressed Chinese manager entered the spacious office.

"Mr. Xenox, sir," he said. "We are ready."

"Come, let us go then," he spoke to another European man, Ulrich Bernoulli, who was comfortably seated in an elegant chair just stubbing out a thin cigarette. He was a financial officer of the UBS AG Bank out of Hong Kong. The three exited the plush office by elevator to a lower floor, crossed a glass encased walkway to an adjacent building and entered the production area of a clean brightly lit factory.

A foreman in blue coveralls and radiating efficiency approached, clipboard in hand. "Mr. Jianguo," he said greeting the manager and conferred momentarily in Chinese.

"As you can see, production has outpaced our expectations," Jianguo explained to Xenox and Bernoulli, who nodded approval. "On last reckoning, this man says we are at least three weeks ahead of schedule."

"Excellent, excellent," Xenox beamed. "How soon can we expect the merchandise in Los Angeles?"

Jianguo conversed rapidly to the foreman. "These boxes are sent to Shanghai where they are integrated with the internal electronics. Within forty-eight hours, after arrival there, the new package will leave Shanghai Pudong by airfreight for California. He says, this week, the first shipment of fifty thousand devices will be at Los Angeles International Airport customs waiting your clearance."

The foreman descended a short metal staircase and signaled to a woman technician who picked up a turquoise blue electrical box and handed it to him. It was a rectangle approximately two feet by one foot by one foot, made of a sturdy all-weather plastic material. It was easy to hold in both hands. He passed it up to Jianguo who in turn handed it to Xenox who examined it closely. It was empty, a casing for more complicated electronics. A sensitive meter dial was incorporated into one of the outer sides, but only a few wires hung loosely on the inside.

"Yes," he stated matter-of-factly. "I knew I could count on you." He handed the box to the banker who felt its weight and passed it back to the foreman. The three retraced their steps to the office to toast the successful conclusion of business. Xenox smiled to himself. Although relations between China and America were strained these days, business must go on.

- - -

At the same moment, some six hundred and fifty miles south in an office at the Shanghai Zhangjiang Technical Park in the Pudong New Economic Area, Bob Redlinger was examining a tidy array of computer board electronics carefully arranged as a single component. He conferred with a Chinese administrator who was explaining to him the intricacy of a systems merging process. He indicated a turquoise blue box on a work table.

(20)

Humidity buffered the jetliner as it bobbled in for an ambiguous but jarring landing. Its widows ran with beads of sweat and its brakes groaned as the jet jerked to a halt before the terminal. A stewardess wrenched the airlock handles and the main passenger door slid open. The remaining pressure in the cabin equalized with the inrush of musky North African air. The arrivals ramp wobbled out and attached loosely to the plane. The passengers filed out without much visible enthusiasm. Most were arriving at Tripoli for business, mostly in oilfield jobs or related construction contracts. Little more than the promise of high wages lured foreigners these days. Colonel Gaddafi's military regime had never especially encouraged the casual travelers. After his horrific demise, it was a practice that the latest powers-to-be saw no reason to change; Libya was still an off-limits country for light-weight tourism.

Kevin moved with the flow, stopping to fill out his disembarkation and currency declaration cards, and then joined the line at passport control. He scanned remnants of the bright green paint that had once lined the arrivals hall walls and proclaimed slogans from The Colonel's Green Book, a manifesto for Libyan modernization and revolution. There seemed to have been a vague catchphrase for every occasion. Painted over but still thinly legible "In Need, Freedom is Latent" awarded Kevin a moment of contemplation. He handed a cubicle officer his passport and papers.

The official glanced at Kevin's photograph, checked the visa validity, and glanced up suspiciously. "You are American," he all but accused.

"Yes," Kevin replied nonchalantly. "North American, Canada, like the passport says." He grinned innocently. The man grudgingly stamped the visa with its entry and expiration dates and waved Kevin through. Kevin dropped his carry-all onto the stainless-steel counter grill and zipped it open for inspection. An apathetic customs soldier pulled out some clothing, prodded a bit inside the bag, made a mark with chalk on its side and shoved it along. Kevin walked into the crowded lobby where he stood visibly alone and expectant.

"Mr. Varyte," a neatly dressed man inquired. "This way please."

The driver drove a compact Honda sedan towards the main highway into town but turned sharply before leaving the airport grounds. He sped cautiously along a modest avenue bordered by tall eucalyptus trees and pink flowered oleander bushes eventually halting at a red and white candy-striped barrier where heavily armed guards idled at a security booth. Kevin caught a glimpse of a tank muzzle protruding from behind yellow buildings with rusty tiled roofs. A barracks atmosphere seemed to languor in the air. A red eyed sentry sauntered up to the car and gestured obnoxiously with his Kalashnikov. Kevin looked the other way.

The driver rattled off a few words in Arabic and handed out a heavily stamped official paper. The guard gave a disinterested look at the foreigner in the passenger seat. The barrier rose and the car drove on.

"What did you tell him?" Kevin asked.

"That you are going to work in the oilfields and your plane is here. Many engineers get their plane from this area of the airport to go into the deep Sahara." Kevin nodded. Moments later, the car emerged from the shady trees and warehouse rows onto concrete. It stopped at a huddle of corrugated metal hangers. Kevin stepped onto oily cement. The driver handed him his bag, pointed to the nearest hanger and without another word, drove back the way he came. Kevin stretched and walked the short sunny distance into the shade and fumes of the hanger. As his eyes adjusted to the gloom, he made out the form of a twin-engine Otter. A hand tool clattered onto the concrete, followed by the familiar sound of English cursing. He ambled towards the commotion and stopped at the wing. A mechanic in greasy coveralls was reaching down from a ladder by the starboard motor, but stopped when he saw Kevin's shoes and looked up.

"'ello, mate. Give us a 'and 'ere, would ya?" he said pointing to the dropped spanner. Kevin picked it up and handed it to the Australian. "Thanks, mate. Yer must be Kevin Varyte. Been expectin' ya." He wiped his hands with an oily rag and extended one, then shook his head. "A bit grimy there," he apologized.

"How are you doing?" Kevin asked at a loss for what else to say.

"Fine, fine. The name's Jack Fillmore, but everyone just calls me Aus, of course," he grinned. "I'm pilot, mechanic and chief garbage collector for this contraption. Keeps me outta trouble. I run out to the fields two, maybe three times a week on average, but I'm on call 24-7."

Kevin looked around. "Yew may as well relax, Kev me boy. We ain't going nowhere till morning. There's a spare bunk in there if yew want to catch some kip." He indicated to a separate office. "The air conditioner works right proper. Just wiggle the wall socket if it don't turn right on."

"That's a rum thing," Kevin said with a wink. "I think I'll do just that." Sweat stained his shirt. "A nice cool down suits me fine. I'll see you this evening when this heat lets up a bit." He entered the room, flicked on the AC, tapped the plug with his foot, and flipped his shoes off. He reclined on a thin hard mattress and let out a long sigh. The heat gradually receded as cool air pumped into the room. He pulled a coarse blanket over himself and drifted wearily asleep.

(21)

Amber coals flickered in a sand pit near the entrance flap of a low black goat hair tent at the Bedouin camp where Chloe was waiting out her second night. The remnants of a nightly feast were spread across coarsely woven colorful carpets lain directly on the sand close to the glowing embers. Several Bedu men slept there. Chloe was restless. She had slept the previous night and rested most of this day in a dingy little room on the upper floor of the bare concrete military building. There was a fan but no air-conditioning. She had stood briefly on the outpost roof around noon and let her eyes drift around the full circumference of desert horizon, seeing nothing in every direction as if blind. The magnificent desolation was overwhelming. The midday sun had been oppressive, but since it set, the air stirred coolly. She felt as if a weight had been lifted from her entire being. As the stars appeared, she had been drawn outside where they glimmered unimaginably, subduing her in a way she had never experienced. She allowed unfamiliar, yet timeless, sensations carry her along the sand towards the Bedu shelters, a nomadic world at whose threshold she could only hover but never enter.

"Tomorrow, perhaps," the driver spoke out of nowhere. Too calm to be startled, Chloe looked at him absently. "Yes," she agreed. "Perhaps tomorrow." She turned and walked back to the outpost block and her room. Army guards were snoring on the veranda as she passed.

- - -

Kevin woke with a claustrophobic jerk and grabbed instinctively for his automatic. It wasn't there. Creeping panic overwhelmed him and he fumbled in desperation for the missing weapon until sleep began to recede. The gun, he had to leave it behind to get here. Here? His mind raced. He glanced anxiously around absorbing a bed, an enclosed room, the hum of an air-conditioner. Malta, he suddenly remembered and relaxed. Libya, he stiffened, and sat up. He flicked a table lamp on, fully conscious, wiped the sweat from his brow and reached for his shoes. He crossed to the door and went out into the warm night air of the airplane hanger.

The Australian was not there. Kevin glanced at his wrist watch. It was after midnight. He walked to the open hanger doors and viewed the airfield. Military aircraft loomed in the distance but there were only a few red ground lights at this end of the airport. No other silhouettes were distinguishable. "Tomorrow," he murmured. He returned to his air-conditioned cot. Morning would come soon enough. He fell gratefully back into sleep.

- - -

Bill Collins stepped out onto the wood block that balanced as a step on the sand at the front door of his trailer. He gazed at the bright orange lights of the derrick and its elongated shadow that was cast hundreds of yards into the desert's darkness. On the drill floor, the Kelly hose wobbled with each stroke of the massive pumps that sent drilling mud surging through it and down the rotating pipe. The steady turning of the rotary table shook the great black rubber hose making it wriggle like a giant captured eel. The driller's brake screeched mournfully, inch by inch, foot by foot as the spinning steel pipe was carefully lowered into the ground. Minute by minute, hour by hour, the hole grew deeper as the drill bit churned through the subterranean formations a mile below.

He shifted his gaze as a meter-long sand snake caught his eye and writhed from under the trailer towards the mechanical noises and lights. He turned and went in. It was some hours since he had received the message.

"Tomorrow," he calculated. "Perhaps."

[22]

Bill received his next message after dawn, this one from Tripoli. The rendezvous was on. He checked the numbers and located them on a company geological survey map to get the general area. The GPS would hone him right in later. He drew out an invisible line, "Just under a hundred miles. I should be able to cover that in a few hours, if the weather holds."

"What's that?" another technician called from a bunk at the far end of the trailer.

"Nothing, Ed. Just thinking out loud. I have to go south this morning to Sedco Rig 25 to work on the gamma-ray scanner."

Bill tapped out an answering message on the keyboard and pressed the special send keys that would automatically jumble it. Since most rig correspondence was regularly scrambled to preserve company information, there was little worry of suspicion

"That oughta be fun," the junior tech answered sympathetically.

"Yeah, well, that's the breaks. They'll be tripping here today for bit change so you'll get some sack time anyway."

"Okay, we'll see you later, Bill. Take care."

- - -

The lone soldier sprawled across the front seat of his vehicle. He woke with a start as his satellite set bleeped. He had kept the instrument within arm's reach on the floor throughout the night. He clutched for the ear set draped over the steering wheel. The message arrived. The Arab unfolded his map and aligned it with his compass. "Fifty kilometers," he nodded.

Bill walked to a blue Toyota Land Cruiser that must have been a prototype left over from the 70's. It was basically a truck. There was little resemblance to the fancy vehicles that had metamorphosed over the years. He checked the survival essentials, GPS, gasoline, oil, water levels, plenty of drinking water, side cans of radiator water and extra gasoline, metal tread pads for deep sand, first aid kit, signal mirror, flashlight, flares, a food tin provided by the camp cook, coffee. All was in order. He climbed aboard and drove over to the oil company man, the senior on-site boss, who was walking towards the derrick for morning inspections.

Bill leaned out the cab window, "Sam, we're having some equipment problems around Sebha. I'm the only one out here who can handle it right now, so I'm heading down there for two or three days. Ed will hold down the fort till I get back."

"Okay, Bill. Do you want someone to go with you?"

"No thanks, Sam. I'll manage. I'll call in when I get there."

"Okee dokee, see you when you get back." Their casual attitudes towards the dangers of Saharan travel were learned through years of experience. There was no point in getting unnecessarily anxious. Things moved at their own pace or not at all. Much was in the hands of Allah, even for foreigners. Bill headed southeast into the trackless wastes that vibrated with the morning heat.

Chloe walked down the concrete steps from the shade of the cinder block terrace. She held her small bag over her shoulder. The driver was waiting. "We go now," he announced. The girl nodded. The air conditioning in the Range Rover felt luxurious after the two nights and the long day in the rough building. She took a last look at the Bedouin camp before the vehicle's motion pulled her eyes away. Within minutes the entire scene had vanished behind an undulating curtain of heat waves.

- - -

The Australian revved the Otter's dual engines, rocking the plane before take off. Kevin squirmed in the co-pilot's seat. A voice from the control tower crackled deafeningly over the airwaves. Kevin lowered the volume of his headset. The voice was in English but was so shrill and heavily accented that Kevin could not distinguish a word. The pilot answered in the same staccato language and released the brakes. The plane rushed into the air, buffeting and twisting, sending pressure creaks through the cabin as it lifted into the sky. "Perhaps, today," Kevin murmured.

(23)

The sun inched higher into the vast sky as the cumbersome planet dodged below it. The sands melted into glass. The air stung. Bill drove with manic concentration, sweat trickling down his forehead, his shirt damp. The glare was smearing his depth perception, low ridges were closer than they appeared, and shallow gullies appeared unexpectedly. He had been driving carefully for three hours and had been growing nervous for the last thirty minutes. The southern horizon was dark and looming closer at a rapid pace.

"Ghibli," he swore. "Damn."

The fierce Sahara sandstorm was notorious for blowing up in a matter of hours to scour everything in its path with a low wall of sand and smother what remained under a mile-high cloud of dust. Unpredictable in their frequency or length, this one had appeared without warning. Bill glanced at his watch and looked at the approaching maelstrom. "I'll never beat it." He headed for a small outcrop of rock, switched off the engine and rolled the windows up tight. He knew this stinging blizzard could last a matter of hours or even days.

- - -

Chloe reached over her shoulder and pulled a bottle of French mineral water from the box on the back seat. She twisted the cap, poured sparkling fluid into a metal cup and took a satisfying swallow. The driver tapped her on the shoulder and pointed to the horizon.

"Ghibli coming. Much sand. Soon we must stop." Chloe looked where the man was indicating. Her eyes flickered momentarily but she said nothing.

- - -

The Otter thrashed about in the erratic gusts of air that loiter delinquently over the desert. Jack jostled Kevin and gestured for him to adjust the volume on his headset and position his neck microphone.

"Ghibli," the pilot announced. He pointed ahead and below. "Worst sandstorms on the face of God's good Earth. I won't be able to land an' git out again before that hits. But don't yew worry none, Kev, me boy, I've come prepared. Ever jump before?"

Kevin felt familiar turns in his stomach as the butterflies grew teeth and tried to gnaw their way out. "Sure," he answered.

"What? Yew gotta speak up. Hold the mic against yer throat. That's right"

"Yeah, I've jumped before. No sweat," Kevin replied calmly as a bead of sweat trickled down his spine.

"Good on ya, mate. There's a chute in back. Yew've got about five minutes."

Kevin disconnected his communications set and seat belts and clambered to the few seats behind the cockpit. He found the parachute neatly stashed near the back door. Without hesitation, he hefted it onto his shoulders and clamped the steel harness clips together. Fighting inertia, he waddled forward and tapped the pilot on the shoulder.

The Australian gave him the thumbs up, flicked a lever and a series of switches and went aft. "Automatic pilot," he shouted and jerked the sliding door open.

Dry hot air rushed in with a flash of unshielded sun. The pilot gripped him by the shoulder, attached a static line from the chute to a clamp on the floor, and shouted, "Good luck. You may have to hunker down a smidge under that storm."

Kevin forced a grin. He took a deep breath, dangled his legs out over the rushing brink, clutched the door rim and pushed himself hard into the void. The pilot yanked in the flapping cord, shoved the door shut and returned to take control of his plane. He would make a stop, or a flyover, if he couldn't land, at one of the oil production sites before returning to Tripoli. It's always safer to have an alibi in these sorts of situations.

[24]

Mr. Papenicholeu greeted Ahmed and Fatima warmly. "Come. Let me show you our little enterprise." He guided the young couple out of his office overlooking a stone wharf at the Athenian port of Piraeus. They stood at one end of an elongated warehouse that was orderly stacked with crates and disassembled machinery.

"We own none of this," the shipping agent proudly proclaimed with an all-encompassing sweep of his hand. "We only move it for others. It's a very lucrative and satisfactory state of affairs, none of the problems of ownership, just the benefits of income."

They walked, chatting towards a bright open doorway that led onto the dockside itself where a white painted, rust streaked freighter was secured. It swayed almost imperceptibly on the slight harbor swell. "So, your father wants you to take an interest in his business?" the Greek remarked slyly.

"Yes," Ahmed answered. "Father asked me to handle this since he is very busy in Cairo."

"That's fine. The sooner you learn the ways of commerce, the better off you will be. But there is not much to this, though," he added leading Ahmed towards a stacked row of crates waiting the loading crane.

"ChemSearch. Dest: Port of Entry: Los Angeles, California, USA," Ahmed read aloud. Some crates were being nailed shut. Ahmed stooped over an open one. He reached in and extracted a shiny, circular metal medallion three inches in diameter and about half an inch thick. There was an intricate filigree cross-like pattern etched onto the front. The back was smooth.

"Indian?" Ahmed inquired. The agent took the piece.

"Afghani or Pakistani, I would guess." He answered. "Very rare, from the mountain tribal areas near the Khyber Pass, I imagine, Baluchistan maybe. They should be appealing considering all the war interest nowadays. I'm surprised some Taliban or Pakhtunkhwa tribesmen didn't seize them along the way. Not precious, by any means, but profitable and chic. They should be well received in America." He tossed the medallion back into the box. A workman nailed the lid shut and signaled a crane operator.

Mr. Papenicholeu placed one hand on Ahmed's shoulder, the other on Fatima's, and spoke. "Come, I will introduce you to the necessary paperwork that accompanies all this business, and give you the documents your father requires. You may sign them for him. Then I will take you out for an authentic Greek feast."

[25]

Chloe pulled the black and white Arab headdress tighter around her mouth and nostrils. Her clothes were caked with dust and breathing was laboriously slow, shallow and careful to avoid choking. She was wet with perspiration. The driver had stopped and shut off the motor when the first dust wave had rolled over them. Without the motor, there was no air-conditioning.

"The sand, very bad for engine," he explained. He had pulled the hood of his military jacket over his head and had handed the Arab argyle cloth to Chloe. "Use this," he said "Wet, like this." He damped a corner of the cloth with mineral water and held it over his mouth. "For breathing."

Chloe did as she was told. They huddled wordlessly as the storm reduced their world to a shaking claustrophobic box. The sun dimmed. Chloe could hardly see the hood in front of the windscreen. Sand and dust had consumed everything.

They waited.

- - -

Bill Collins reclined on the front seat of the small Toyota truck. He wore a dust mask and welding goggles. He was soaked in sweat and swatted occasionally at swirling dust rivulets that eked through every gap and fissure as if they were flies. He whistled to himself and watched the minutes tick by on his watch. "Better late than never." He waited.

- - -

The soldier coughed from the dust inside his beat-up Land Rover. A back window was missing and he had tried to cover the open space with part of a tarpaulin. He was only partially successful in his efforts. "At least I won't have to drive after this right away," he thought to himself. He was already at the rendezvous coordinates and had been for hours. He had heard an airplane minutes before the sand hit and blotted out the sky. Now he could only wait.

- - -

Kevin curled himself in a fetal crouch under his camouflaged rip-stop nylon parachute when the wall of dust and sand reached his spot and engulfed him in chaos. He had landed safely, though surprisingly firmly, on a shallow dune and had merely minutes to wave as Jack swooped the Otter above him waggling its wings.

The Australian literally was in a race with the wind. Kevin now tugged at the loose ends of his fragile tent while the wind struggled to rip it from his grasp. He could feel the weight of sand building up around his back. "Great," he said spitting dust from his mouth and trying not to crunch sand between his teeth. "To be buried alive, that's all I need." He huddled in as comfortable a position as possible to wait out the tempest.

- - -

An early morning mist slithered across the glass surface of a small pond. Feathery wisps of gold trailed over the dark surface. The rising sun was radiant but barely warmed the cool air. It was quite refreshing. Dew lay thick on the grass. Lindsey Merric paused in his jogging to perform a brief stretching routine, then zipped up his collar and continued along the trodden path. Events were in motion "over there" and there was little to do in the meantime but wait.

[26]

The main entrance courtyard of Cairo's sprawling Khan el Khalili Souk was teeming as usual. Taxis trundled along the Sikkit al-Badistand bumper to bumper, choking engines nuzzled against coughing exhausts in the stifling afternoon warmth. The sidewalks fared no better. Sweating pedestrians jostled to maintain their places on the crowded pavements. Merchandise moved along at a snail's pace, on top of heads, under arms, on backs, in donkey carts, in overburdened trucks, on bicycles. Anything that could serve to carry was utilized. Brilliant sunlight glossed the painted shop signs bordering the square, causing the dust to flicker in the air at the entrance passageways to the myriad of tourist shops that dimmed into a labyrinth of shadows and shady dealings. The ancient origins of the Souk date as far back as 1382 with the building of a great caravanserai that helped secure the foundations for Cairo's market tradition of wealth and trade. It had also been an early center of subversive activities. The most recent incident occurred in April a few years back with the self-detonation of a suicide bomber that killed a score of people. It had taken some time for the tourist trade to return to normal.

At one far corner of the crowded plaza, just visible at a turn of the sidewalk, an ordinary shop window glinted garishly with the customary selections of brass ornaments, silver and gold, alabaster carvings, ornate lanterns, imitation papyrus, intricately inlaid boxes and tables, semiprecious jewelry, water pipes, an endless medley of merchandise. The store was stuffed with traditional trinkets from floor to ceiling. The sweet sickly odor of incense lingered around the doorway. It was trapped in place by a canopy of canvass and the humid air that hovered over the bazaar. It was an invisible presence, a crippling cloud of decadence.

The man gazing intently through binoculars from behind a wrought iron balcony grate across the square was a thin man, skeletal to the point of emaciation. Pallor appeared to have been permanently slavered onto his tan skin from whence it leaked into his eyes. He could not smell the aroma, but he sensed its presence.

Such a fragrance had once heralded his disappearance into an opaque world that few returned from, the smoky dreamland of hashish and opium. At the threshold of vanishing forever into addiction, something inside him rebelled. He chose substance over evaporation and revived with a vengeance.

He now existed entirely for revenge. It was invigorating to settle the score with the living who, as he perceived it, had nearly smothered him to death and now crowded in on his rightful space in life. He lowered the binoculars, paced nervously, then checking himself, sat calmly down in a wicker chair positioned with a clear view over the square. He took a sip of thick gahwa saada, plain Egyptian coffee, from a delicate cup and glanced at his ornate watch.

In the shop, the air was indeed stiflingly perfumed, although it was cool and comfortable. A sweating air-conditioner struggled with the heat outside that was merely a frequent power failure at bay. Ali Muhammad Mahmoud, Ahmed's father, drank another glass of tea in the traditional style, through a sugar cube between his teeth. He sat in an elaborate chair in a plush little antechamber reserved for well heeled tourists. Across a mother of pearl freckled table top, a heavier, white-haired man sat in robes. They were talking animatedly.

"I tell you; it was the best thing to do," Mahmoud said. "If I had gone myself there would be immediate suspicion. I was just in Athens in April, and again in May, and again now? No, my friend, trust me. It would be too much. My son knows nothing of these matters. To him it is a vacation, a break from the army. He even has his fiancée along with him."

"But many things can go wrong..." the white-haired man began but was interrupted.

"He thinks the shipment is a load of Balucchi medallions which is what they are meant to resemble. Importing them from Yemen just makes him think there's something illegal about the process. All he knows is that I want to avoid customs duties."

"Ah, yes, my brother, I am sure you are right," the other answered. "I worry needlessly. It is a habit, this caution and worry."

"It is often difficult to distinguish between the two," Ali Muhammad agreed.

The entry door opened with a jangle of bells. A delivery man came in with a medium sized cardboard box. The white-haired shopkeeper rose. "Just set it here on the table," he said, indicating towards Mahmoud.

"More junk, I'm sure. The season is just beginning its peak. I won't be a moment." He exited the store with the delivery guy.

Ali Muhammad sank into his chair and reflected. This was the last time; he had told his Muslim Brotherhood contacts. He was growing older and weary of the risks. He had already given them a useful lifetime of smuggling whatever was important for the cause, guns, ammunitions, explosives, and even heroin to increase finances, but recently the causes seemed more confused, more difficult to understand and most importantly more difficult to believe in.

Sometimes he longed for the straightforwardness of the old Nasser days. The military regime had been oppressive, of course, but they had always had that one unifying hope, the dream that the United Arab Republic would somehow seize the leadership of a grand pan-Arab state, making Cairo and Misr itself, the focal of third world powers stretching from Malaysia to Morocco. Not only would the British and Americans be put in their place, but so would the Chinese and the Soviets.

Egypt had been well positioned for the role in the 1950's and 60's and had effectively and lucratively fleeced the great empires of millions of pounds, dollars and rubles of aid money by unpredictably alternating favors and penalties. But those days were long gone and these days were much different.

With all these problems, he thought, Iraq and Iran, Afghanistan, Lebanon, Gaza and the West Bank. And then, the Arab Spring Revolution with its chaotic legacy, all crowned by the Islamic State in Syria and the Levant. And the cherry on top? Normalization with Israel of all things! Unthinkable half a generation ago. Impossible.

It was difficult to tell who was who anymore; Hamas, Hezbollah, al Qaida, The Revolutionary Guards, the Arab Unification Party? What did it all mean? The Brotherhood was especially under political attack. You couldn't even know which faction was on top or, worst yet, who was friendly. Some were pushing for more militancy and communist influences, like those tied to the Iraqis and As-Sa'iqa with its Syrian leanings. With so many vying factions there was no longer a center or a coherent path ahead. Nor would there ever be, he thought to himself, at least not in my lifetime.

Unity was a hopeless dream, so why continue the struggle? Yes, I have done enough. It is time for me to retire. This, he had told his superiors and they had not argued nor tried to dissuade him. They had simply nodded to each other reluctantly.

The shopkeeper and the delivery man stood briefly blinking in the sun before rapidly crossing the square. They knew they were being closely scrutinized. The gaunt man saw them pass. He quickly rose to his feet and pressed a series of numbers on a cell phone. Within seconds, a cloud of dense smoke and glass billowed unexpectedly from the plaza tourist shop, followed momentarily by a muffled explosion. It was a slow-motion scene hardly noticeable from this distance, but police whistles were already mingling with the cries of the crowd.

(27)

Xandrieu Xenox swiveled around from his forty-eighth-floor panorama of the New York City morning and focused his attention on the two Middle Easterners seated before his desk. "Yes, China certainly is lovely this time of year, but it is good to be back in America," he mused envisioning his recent immersion into Beijing's dense smog. His guests nodded. The heavy oak door opened and a pretty Lebanese secretary entered.

"Excuse me," she interrupted politely and handed her boss a message. "This came in last night."

When the door closed behind the girl, he explained, "More trinkets have cleared Athens and are en route to Los Angeles, an interesting side line of mine, nothing of importance. Now, we were discussing Euro refinancing investments in Dubai when we last met, I believe. It was the expansion cancellation at Jebel Ali that has you worried?"

- - -

Ahmed motioned for Fatima to walk further back. He could not get her and the entire Acropolis in the viewfinder together if she stood so close. The shutter clicked and a Greek boy offered to take another picture with both of them in it. Ahmed swung her around happily for the camera. He gave the boy a euro and retrieved his camera.

"I'm so happy," Fatima laughed. "Must we return so soon?"

"I'm afraid so," Ahmed answered. "I have to report in to my commander day after tomorrow and I still have all the paperwork to give to father."

"Race," the girl called and the two tripped off down the rough stone path to the city below.

[28]

The Ghibli sandstorm died as rapidly as it had arisen, leaving an uncanny tranquil hush in its wake. As the suffocating dark wall of sand retreated towards the horizon, a freshly swept desert scene was exposed under the dimming afternoon sun. A smothered groan rose from a trivial lump of sand. It shuddered as camouflaged rip-stop nylon fabric broke the surface. Kevin moaned and flung the parachute aside. It was not just another lull, this time the storm had expired.

He stood up, shaking grit from his clothes, and coughed and spit sand. "Three and a half hours. God, what a place." He was unaware of his good fortune; it had only been a mild blow. It could easily have lasted three and a half days.

He reached into a zipper pocket and took out a small bleeper. Checking the three hundred and sixty degrees of horizon revealed only the receding cloud to the northeast. He pressed the only button on the small transmitter and waited doubtfully. Some fifty kilometers away, the soldier saw the signal light on his communications set. He flicked a transmission switch that crunched with encrusted sand. The electronic devise in Kevin's hands blinked a red eye. Kevin sighed and reclined onto the parachute. "At least I'm not alone out here."

The soldier started his engine. He could home in on the signal easily now. "Not far," he assured himself.

- - -

"Hot damn it," Bill cursed and kicked the side of his Toyota, "Alone out here!" He had just heard the signal bleeps that he knew were the communications between his Arab agent and this Kevin Varyte guy, and now this useless pile of junk vehicle was threatening to leave him stranded. He opened the hood and removed the carburetor cover. It was clogged with sand. So was the oil filter.

"Great," he moaned. "This could take hours. Well, better late than not at all."

- - -

Chloe stood next to the Range Rover dusting herself off and shaking sand from her hair. The driver patiently dug sand accumulations away from the wheels. The vehicle was practically buried on one side. Chloe watched the storm disappearing in the distance. Never had she seen a land quite as violent and detached as this. She thought back to the Bedouin camp and the child who had pointed the empty gun at her. She walked towards a small dune and stretched. She expected to return immediately but the emptiness carried her on a way more and then a bit further. She was surprised when she heard an engine cough back to life and startled when she turned around to see the distance she had walked. The driver beeped the horn, waved and drove the half mile to reach her.

She climbed onto her seat with a dazed expression. "Here drink some more," the man said giving her a full bottle of water as all four wheels lurched forward. He pressed the air-conditioning lever on and a cloud of dust blew out onto Chloe's lap. She gave the man a hard glance, but it went unnoticed.

(29)

Kevin stood with the Arab soldier in deep sand by the dilapidated green Land Rover as the sunset saturated the sky with orange. A vehicle was rapidly approaching trailing an immense cloud of sun hued dust. They watched expectantly as it grew more visible, first distinguishing its blue color, then its pick-up size. It arrived with a soft slide of tires.

Bill jumped out and extended his hand. "Greetings, Kevin Varyte, I presume?" he shouted boisterously and laughed. "Bloody Ghibli clogged up my motor, almost didn't make it."

"Well, it's good you're here now," Kevin answered shaking the man's hand. "Obeid, here, found me before I had a chance to panic. I had a bit of a rough landing though, I must admit. I just curled up under the chute and tried to keep breathing."

Bill glanced at the ruffled bundle of nylon a few paces away and grunted, "Not the most hospitable place is the Sahara. We'd better bury this in any case."

He procured a shovel from the truck and began to toss sand over the fabric. "No need to explain why any of us has a parachute with us," he said between shovelfuls. "Our Sparrow is headed for the Sebha Oasis area apparently."

"Apparently," Kevin agreed. "But what's there?"

"Well, we're not really sure. It's calmed down recently. That's why we're here again, petrol business as normal. We spend half our time waiting in the wings. The town was quite a mess during the 2011 Revolution. Now it's a new regime.

"There are over two hundred thousand people for starters; it's a city really, where the late Colonel proclaimed his sixties revolution. There's also a fort, military installations, and the like. We're a good way northeast at the moment, somewhere between Wadi al Shati and Al Jufrah. We've got an exploration well sinking pipe some twenty kilometers from Sebha in the same direction. We'll be headed there. We thought about bringing you in as a tourist first. There are some amazing sights here, Lake Gaberoun, for one."

"Lake?" Kevin raised his eyebrows.

"Yep, salt though," Bill answered. "Unusual geology around here. Then, there's an oasis string, the El Mandara, Mafo Lake and Un Almaa. We're also at the edge of the Awabari Sand Sea, dunes hundreds of feet high. The place is still popular with adventure tourists, mostly European. But that would leave a pretty conspicuous paper trail of visas and permits on you.

"Then we have the illegals from Sudan and other places down south trying to get across the Med to Europe via Tripoli. They all come through here. And that stirs up plenty of police and army activity. So, we thought we'd just get you here by the scenic route."

"It's appreciated, I'm sure," Kevin responded, thinking of the hours under the parachute as the sandstorm wailed.

"Thanks," Bill chuckled. "Actually, it is great cover, working the oilfield. People worry about climate change, but the world has to keep going on."

Kevin nodded, "Apparently so."

"There're lots of people involved out here, Russians, French, Italians, and so on, so you've no problems blending in. Plus, for me, there's the extra income, nobody can live off what the government doles out. Oh, by the way, I'm a well monitoring technician and you'll be my assistant."

He tossed the shovel in the back of the Toyota truck and turned to Obeid talking in Arabic. The soldier answered, nodded to Kevin, stepped into the Land Rover and drove off in a southwesterly direction. They watched the vehicle momentarily before climbing into the Toyota. The bright blue truck had turned a dull purple as the sunset reddened. The air now stirred with a hint of night.

Bill set a course slightly further east, carefully revved the engine, and cautiously inched forward. "We don't want to spin the tires. Even with four-wheel drive I've seen some of these guys sink up to the chassis. It's a real hassle to pull them out; all comes from spinning the tires. You just keep digging in deeper. If you get the momentum going first, then you're alright."

Kevin seemed interested, so he continued. "I've seen sand highways out here that you wouldn't even know are there, 'til one of these Bedu drivers points 'em out. And sure enough, you look a little closer and you see you're on a four-lane expressway, all sand, with tracks going off into a sea of dunes, nearly invisible, but with specific destinations like roads anywhere."

"Fascinating," Kevin replied.

"It certainly is," Bill said. "We're on one now." He switched the headlights on. Kevin looked out the windscreen but saw only sand and an evening star. There was no road.

"As my assistant," Bill picked up his earlier train of thought, "we'll be able to get in as close as we like to Sebha.

"I don't know much about oil well monitoring," Kevin said thoughtfully.

"You won't need to. Just remember at the well ask only me questions. But if anyone corners you, just say you're working on the computer." Bill laughed, "The computer and electronics scare the hell out of everyone. They'll leave you alone."

"And how will this help us get in close?" Kevin asked perplexed.

"Well, the rig's not many miles from Sebha," Bill answered.

"We'll find an excuse to go into town if it becomes necessary. The rig crews go in from time to time anyway to have a look around."

Kevin nodded. "And this girl? How do we find her?"

"Good question. We just wait and listen now. Obeid is going in. He'll signal us if anything's going on. Meanwhile, I'll try to educate you about the damn drilling business, bring you up to speed a bit on well operations." He laughed heartily.

[30]

Lindsey Merric sat at his desk and fiddled with his pencil. He brushed a heap of paper aside, got up and absently reached for the golf putter that leaned against a well-stocked oak and glass bar. He tapped the white ball that lay on the floor and watched as it rolled soundlessly across the grey office rug and tinkled into a whiskey glass tipped on its side by the door.

- - -

Ahmed Mahmoud stood beside his mother and younger brother and sister in the full glare of the sun. The summit stones of one of the Giza pyramids were visible amongst the concrete and palm fronds of the background. All were dressed in the black of formal mourning. He tried vainly to comfort his mother who sobbed behind a dark veil. A number of his father's business acquaintances and friends of the family were grouped solemnly nearby. Fatima waited on the opposite side with her future mother-in-law holding her hand. The merchant, Ali Muhammad, lay placid and seemingly contented in his modest coffin. The mullah read his final words from the Koran and gave a slight signal with his fingers. The coffin was closed and lowered with due care into its grave at the desert's edge. Ahmed shuddered as his mother began to wail uncontrollably.

- - -

Kevin trudged up the metal grill step ladder to the drill floor in the midday heat. He was dressed in shorts, Redwing steel tip oil resistant leather boots and silver hard hat. He felt a strange elation as he gazed into the shimmer where a thin line of green trees marked the outskirts of Sebha Oasis. The driller in his metal doghouse stopped the rotating pipe and pulled on a worn cord that sounded a dull whistle. Three roughnecks clambered to their stations to make a pipe connection. They grasped the heavy yellow tongs and swung them around the drill string. The driller hydraulically tightened the connecting wire ropes that clenched the tongs and then broke the Kelly circulation head from the pipe as if with giant wrenches. A burst of drilling mud drenched the floor as a roughneck wrestled the Kelly to the side. A new joint of pipe was added and tightened, lowered and reconnected with the Kelly hose. The driller spun the rotary table and the mud pumps resumed their throbbing. The drill string screeched as a few inches descended into the hole and the roughnecks disappeared below. Kevin watched with rare fascination.

- - -

Dean leaned against the counter in a spacious warehouse and waited as a Los Angeles Port customs official pried a board off a crate. The uniformed girl reached in and took out a circular silver medallion, a few inches in diameter. She held it up to the light to get a closer look at the carved pattern on one side. It wasn't precious metal by any means.

"Trinkets?" she questioned.

Dean shrugged. "Tourism is big business these days. Architectural art it says on the invoice. Guess that's why there are so many of them."

(31)

The stars floated in the inky sky over the low narrow mud walls that protected a group of dwellings on the fringes of the oasis. Heavy clumps of dates hung overhead in dust crusted palms and swayed in a gentle breeze. Obeid crouched beside his Land Rover in the deep shadows of a ruined villa. He wondered if it might have been the home of a wealthy landowner who had eventually fled the country in the wake of the September 1969 coup and the subsequent socialist reforms. He tapped furtively on his communications set.

- - -

Kevin lay on his bunk and thumbed through one of the many spiral-ring engineering manuals that filled the shelves in the rig camp trailer. He reckoned he had been there about four days. Drilling was slow and uneventful. He wondered how the workers maintained their sanity in such a stultifying place.

Bill explained with a resigned grin. "No problem, just ask some of the Philippine cooks or the Indonesian, Thai, Pakistani, Malay laborers. They're only here for a year or two, not too bad considering after the first six months they'll get a weekend off in Tripoli."

Kevin grimaced.

"Still, they go home relatively wealthy. Actually, the European and American expats rarely stay longer than a month at a time. I'm a tech so I always have an excuse to stay as long as I like. It's quite civilized when you factor in cost of living and hardship bonuses."

Bill flipped over another three cards, frowned and rearranged them. "Well at least my luck at solitaire is improving."

The computer on the desk next to a wall of instruments gave a long buzz followed by three short ones, and repeated the sequence.

"That's it," Bill announced. "Obeid's signal." He checked the time. "Let's go."

[32]

Bill approached the rubble cautiously and eased into the shadows with only the Toyota's parking bulbs lighting the way. Bill blinked those off, on and then off. Dim lights responded ahead. "Obeid," Bill said in a low voice. They moved towards the rendezvous. The three men huddled between the two shadow shrouded vehicles.

"She is here tonight," the Arab whispered. "The woman with the gold hair, the one you call Sparrow."

"You are certain it is her?" Kevin intervened.

"It is her. For three days, she waits. Today she meets some officers of Libyan army, some others, Palestinians, Brotherhood maybe."

"What else?" Bill prompted.

"Tonight, they inspect equipment at a warehouse. Tomorrow, she go. Come, follow with me," he said opening the door.

They drove off in Obeid's vehicle along a dirt track, skirting the shadows of darkened mud dwellings, going deeper into the oasis towards lighted windows, concrete houses and paved roads. Obeid eventually parked in an alleyway uncomfortably near the Sebha Fort, but protected from view by a bulky garbage heap. A large concrete storehouse with corrugated steel roofing was sandwiched between smaller buildings and a barracks.

"Warehouse," Obeid informed Kevin and Bill pointing.

Barbed wire stretched away from the warehouse towards the barracks where a heavily protected check point barricaded the road into the fort. The warehouse was outside of the perimeter and merited only a small security post where a guard in tan uniform talked with the driver of a black limousine. Kevin couldn't read the Arabic numbers on the license plate, but he noticed there were only two, indicating high governmental rank. The driver handed a cigarette out the window and extended a lighter. A nicotine cloud wafted into the glow that shone from the little hut.

"She is already here," Kevin whispered.

"And who else?" Bill wondered.

They waited attentively watching the scene. Ten, twenty minutes passed. Another cigarette appeared. It was close to an hour when the metal door to the warehouse opened with a muted squeal. The guard dropped his third cigarette and snapped to attention clutching the Kalashnikov that hung from his shoulder. A uniformed officer stepped out accompanied by a man in less formal attire. Another military man paused inside the doorway to allow a young woman to step into the night. Her hair hung loosely to her shoulders and glinted gold under the guardhouse light. A breeze stirred the strands of flaxen hair briefly creating an aura around her.

"Beautiful." Kevin murmured to himself.

The group stooped into the limousine and vanished from sight. The driver executed a tight U turn and passed onto the road away from the fort in the direction of the town. "This way," Obeid whispered urgently.

The three back tracked down the alley, dodged around a corner and sprinted through the shadows invisible to the guard house. Obeid led them along the warehouse wall to an obscure door that was bolted and padlocked but balanced on hinges without pins. The Arab pulled the door open just enough for the men to squeeze through. Inside, Bill flicked on a rubber encased flashlight and handed Kevin a small penlight. "Look around," he said casting the beam in a wide arc.

Heavy equipment, bits and pieces of the international war machines, was stashed everywhere. Tank treads and metal wheels were neatly stacked alongside large muzzled gun barrels and rounds of cannon ammunition.

"Not surprising," Kevin commented quietly. He stepped silently across the hard dirt floor. Wooden boxes were piled purposefully through most of the building, with pallets of Israeli Uzi machine guns even, dismantled Russian and Czech automatic rifles, M-16s, grenades, bazookas, unending crates of ammunition.

"So, what else is new." He breathed.

Bill hissed. "Take a look at these." Kevin poked his light into an open crate, reached in and removed a pale red rectangular block. It was about eight by six by two inches as far as he could tell. It had a circular indentation in the center of one side, about three inches in diameter. He roughly measured with his finger. It felt compact and heavy.

"Some kind of explosive sealed in a plastic resin coating?" he whispered.

"It seems so," Bill nodded. "That's an odd shape though."

"Unusual," Kevin agreed.

Bill flashed his light down the length of the warehouse. "This whole side is packed to the roof with crates of these things. There must be thousands, tens of thousands, maybe more," he said softly.

Kevin was thoughtful. "Explosives, guns, ammo, etcetera, etcetera. So what? This is a military supply dump."

Obeid interrupted with a nudge. "We go now."

Bill was in agreement. "Yep, we've seen all there is to see here."

Kevin went to replace the pale red block, but he kept hold of it at the last second. He slipped it into his jacket pocket. "I doubt if one will be missed," he murmured.

The Arab held the door ajar as the two Americans squirmed outside. He replaced the door and slipped the two pins back into the hinges and tapped them quietly with his fist. They hastily retraced their steps to the Land Rover and Obeid drove directly back to the ruined villa where the hidden Toyota was safely parked. Kevin waited as Bill conferred with Obeid. The technical engineer then turned the vehicle into the desert where far away the needle glow of the derrick's lights was barely discernible. It was a tiny marker on an invisible line dividing sky from sand.

Obeid somberly watched the truck meld with the night. Fifteen minutes passed while he watched the red glow of the tail lights dimming and bouncing over the invisible desert terrain. When he considered the vehicle to be a safe distance from the oasis city, Bill switched on his headlights. As soon as the Arab soldier saw the white glow appear in the distance, he turned his Land Rover around and drove off in the opposite direction

The Wind

(33)

The wind coursed roughly through the trees on the Langley grounds tugging at clusters of ocher leaves. It was still early in autumn and they clung stubbornly to the flexing branches. A decorative row of evergreens swayed with the gusts.

"And that's it?" Sheldon fumed slapping his ballpoint on the conference table. Lindsey winced at the sharp sound. "Guns and explosives? And now she's returned to her old Zurich to Frankfurt to Beirut schedule, twice a month, Monday there, Friday back, as if nothing happened?"

"And nothing has," Scott reminded him.

"Except for two murder attempts and three dead assassins."

"Yeah, well, we're working on that."

"But it doesn't make sense," Sheldon complained. He liked everything to be laid out logically in predictable formats, as if life had some specific plan or reason.

"What does?" Scott philosophized.

"Okay, okay," Lindsey mediated. A silence, disturbed only by an uneasy shuffling of papers, settled over the table where the small task force had reconvened. "Something is missing," he murmured. "Why the deaths?"

"It could be anything. Most people don't like being followed. Old enemies?" Gloria asked.

"Oh, I doubt that," Lindsey answered. "This appears as if some trouble was taken to keep us from knowing the little that we do know. The odd thing is it appears we were following a dead-end trail anyway."

"So, Kevin's specific identity might still be safe, since he wasn't disturbed in Libya?" Sheldon wondered.

"That mirrors my thoughts, Shel," Lindsey agreed. "They must have lost the trail in Malta or perhaps at Tripoli? But I think for prudence's sake we'll keep Kevin out of this for a spell. Meanwhile, let's keep an eye out for patterns. We're obviously not seeing something here."

"I guess not," Scott agreed. "We'll just have to keep Sparrow under surveillance from a safe distance until something breaks."

"Yes," Lindsey said. "Thank you, gentlemen. Gloria, make sure you can reach us all in this matter if it becomes necessary." The group disbanded, again inconclusively, to deal with other tasks.

[34]

The glass door revolved ponderously counterclockwise causing a prism of lights to flutter across Ahmed's face. He stooped to lift the bags of a middle-aged tourist and his overweight wife. "Did you enjoy your stay in Los Angeles," he asked mechanically with more than a hint of foreign disdain. Though Egyptian children study English on a regular basis, there was no veiling his thick Mediterranean accent. He ushered the couple into a waiting taxi and humbly accepted his tip. A 747 rumbled overhead. LAX was close, less than five miles away. He glanced at his Seiko. His shift was already over. He waved to the front desk and headed towards a side exit. He crossed the parking lot and knocked on a lower-level door. At least he had been able to secure a modest room reserved for employee staff when he was hired with the help of counterfeit documents obtained in Cairo.

"Ahmed?" a timid voice called from within.

"Yes. It's me." The door creaked open. He angrily flung his uniform jacket on the bed and paced by the curtained window. "It has been nearly three months since father was murdered. Three months!"

"Yes, and see how our lives have changed in so short a time," Fatima replied bitterly.

"Those boxes in Athens were addressed to here. There must be a connection between that shipment and father's death. I know it."

"And if there is?" Fatima demanded intensely. "If there is, what can we do?"

Ahmed was slightly subdued. "I don't know," he whispered, "but it's all we have to go on. There were no clues left at home."

Fatima slumped on the bed and rocked herself slowly. "I wish we hadn't come here. I wish it was all like it was before."

"So, do I, but we have to try," he said blankly. He brushed aside the heavy curtain and gazed across the dismal parking spaces at a characterless building. "The company is somewhere north of here in Ventura. I have two days off. I'm going there tomorrow."

(35)

Kevin paused with his tray and reached for an Earl Grey tea bag. The girl behind the counter smiled and handed him a small stainless-steel pot brimming over with steaming water. He returned the smile warmly. Easing himself between the wall and a matronly lady who blocked his way, he shuffled over to a table where two pretty English secretaries sat with a junior employee of the American Embassy in London. Kevin greatly appreciated the café on premises.

The young man looked up as Kevin approached. "Ah ha," he called out jovially. "Look who's here, our wandering boy, Kevin Varyte."

"Hi," Kevin offered joining the party.

"'ello luv," the girls chorused.

"We were just debating the finest place you could ask for to spend a holiday," the young man said. "I say, it's the Caribbean hands down."

"Ah, yes, the Caribbean," Kevin reminisced. "But I'll take the Mediterranean any day." He envisioned the bubbles, the blue water and the small cave in Malta and Sylvia with a grin.

"The Carib, the Med, you can have them both," one of the girls cooed. "For me, it's Bermuda."

Kevin's pager vibrated. "Oh no. Now what?" he moaned. He read the call identification code and moaned again. "Excuse me ladies and ..."

"Jim."

"Right. Well, I've got to take this one in private," he said rising to make a quick exit. He pushed through the door into the hallway and ducked into an elegant wooden in-house telephone booth. He smiled at a gorgeous young lady passing by with an armful of documents and pulled the glass partition shut. He picked up the phone and pressed zero. The operator answered immediately.

"Kevin Varyte. I have a call?" he asked.

"One moment, sir." The operator was audible in the back ground, "Hello, Washington, Mr. Varyte is on the line."

Lindsey Merric's voice came through the secure line. "Kevin?"

"Yes, Mr. Merric," Kevin answered in a resigned tone. A weary expression crossed his face. "Good to hear you again, Mr. Merric. How are you?"

Lindsey looked out his office window at a low grey sky full of cold gusts and drizzle. "Fine," he answered cheerily. "Beautiful sunny fall morning we're having here. It's a bit of an Indian summer, very nice indeed."

Kevin could see across the hallway where a window revealed another dismal English afternoon of darkening sky and steady rain. "What a coincidence," he all but chirped. "We're having a lovely warm stretch here as well. It must have come over from Paris."

Lindsey, smoldering slightly by now, got straight down to business. "Our Sparrow has flown off course again," he said. "She broke routine and flew to LAX instead of Beirut. We're putting you back on that project, priority one. Let's see how quickly you can get out to California. You will be met at the airport, of course."

"Of course," Kevin mimicked carefully.

"Oh, and Kevin," Lindsey paused as if thinking.

"Yes, Mr. Merric?"

"Have a nice day." The telephone clicked off. Kevin waited momentarily listening to the buzz tone, then hung up and stepped into the hall. Jim and the two girls were just leaving the cafeteria, laughing. They saw Kevin who answered their looks with, "Have a nice day, top priority," and retreated down the hall. Three hours later, he was at Heathrow's modern Terminal 5 building waiting to board an evening British Airways Boeing 777-200 direct flight to Los Angeles.

[36]

Mr. Xenox talked animatedly on his telephone. "You have done exceedingly well," he exclaimed. "This opens the door to contracts in all major cities in America. City traffic authorities across the country have already signed for our service, pending the receipt of federal stimulus allocations for traffic safety, of course. This is excellent news." He laid the phone in its cradle and pressed the intercom button. "Get me Hank Bellard in Ventura," he said when the secretary answered. He waited patiently as the numbers connected and the call was passed through the receptionist at the far end of the line.

"Hello, Hank Bellard. Mr. Xenox?" the voice answered.

"This is Xenox. Bellard, the traffic stimulus bill passed through both houses of Congress this week."

"Good news," Hank called out. "That's great."

"Yes, it is," the Greek tycoon agreed. "We can now step-up production to full capacity. The delivery of components will be doubling by the first weeks of November."

"Yes, sir. We have been expecting a demand increase and we are ready for it. Our increased truck flow will blend in with the local industrial oilfield traffic in the area and draw no unwanted attention."

"Good," Xenox replied. "Did Miss Ashley arrive safely?"

Hank looked at the stunning young lady sitting across from his desk. "Yes, sir. She is right here."

"Let me speak with her," Xenox's voice demanded. Hank motioned to Chloe and pressed the speaker tab.

She stood and walked closer to the desk unit. "Hello, Xandrieu."

"You were at the Chicago office, Miss Ashley?"

"Of course, sir," she said with a buttery inflection. "Just yesterday."

"And...?"

"And last week, Miami, and Atlanta, Houston, Albuquerque, Phoenix ..."

Xenox cut her off. "Yes, yes," he said and paused. "Well?"

"Everything is proceeding according to your agenda," Chloe answered confidently. "Everyone seems to be right up with their timetables. There may be some delivery bottlenecks in the near future but nothing of major concern."

Xenox absorbed the information. "Excellent, keep up the good work, Miss Ashley." The line shut off.

Hank and Chloe looked briefly at each other, nothing needed saying. Chloe sighed and walked to the wet bar and diluted her vodka drink with more tonic. She dropped in an orange slice and a fresh ice cube. Hank sipped his whiskey.

"As we were saying," he said indicating a blueprint diagram. "The simplicity of it all is its most fascinating aspect." He picked up a sturdy turquoise blue plastic box and gave it a rap with his knuckles. "Four season all-weatherproof plastic."

It had dimensions of two feet by one foot by one foot with a meter dial on the top surface. "A little bulky," he explained, it required two hands to hold comfortably, "but not too weighty." He tossed it up a few inches. "As you know, the shells are manufactured in China, and the internal components come from elsewhere, but we're assembling the unit right here in California. I'm not mistaken in assuming that you haven't seen a completed one yet?"

"True, I've just been going around checking on pieces, apparently."

"I keep this one in my office as a demo model," Hank continued. "It isn't hermetically sealed like the final product will be." He placed it firmly on his desk and gently pulled the blue cover hood up and off the device. Two wires extended from the hookups beneath the dial and joined with the electronic mechanism connectors below. There were also wires from an external solar cell panel located above the dial.

"Vibrations are visually checked up here," he tapped the meter dial. "This solar panel provides a trickle charge that will keep the unit battery running indefinitely. And down here," he indicated the electronics, "are highly sensitive spring activated detection devices and, of course, electronic chip recording cards."

"Which...?" Chloe questioned.

"Which keep continuous digital recordings that are later translated into statistical and pattern graphs for whatever traffic projection requirements a city might have."

"Neat," Chloe commented. "Very impressive."

"Thanks," Bellard replied. "I designed it myself."

"But won't the data be overwhelming?"

"Nope, the real beauty of this system is that a technician simply carries a recording wand which downloads the information stored on the card. He points the wand at the device, doesn't even have to get out of his truck. The information in the meter is simultaneously wiped clean which provides a fresh start every month and keeps information from overloading on the chips. Then the wand is downloaded into the central computer base. The registers can also be accurately calibrated to only register stress and vibrations over or under certain limits. If officials want to check on heavy truck traffic, they set the readings to ignore automobiles, or vice versa."

Chloe sipped her drink and intently studied the object on Bellard's desk. "So, you could conceivably distinguish the type of traffic you're measuring and maybe even the loads?"

"Exactly, say if someone was looking for suspiciously heavy items being moved about on the interstate system, they would definitely register depending on the settings."

"And this?" she asked.

"That is the heart of the matter." There was a separate section next to the mechanics and electronics, tri-colored and sealed in clear plastic. It took up a great portion of the internal space. "Like the outer cover, this will be sealed airtight in the final version." He opened the pack and removed three equal sized blocks, eight by six by two inches each. They were all pale colored, one green, one red and one blue.

"This outer green block contains an electronically sensitive jelly compound, used for vibration and pressure detection. It provides the basic impulses that are to be monitored and recorded. The inner blue block is the battery, the rechargeable electrical power itself. Now, sandwiched between these two is the special red insulation block. Its function is to keep electronic pulses from jumping across from the battery and interfering with the pressure detection block."

Some of this seemed vaguely familiar to Chloe, but she had seen quite a few parts and pieces over the last several months. "I see," she said simply.

"Recessed between the battery and the insulation block, in the center, fits a round electronic disc like this one." Bellard removed a silver disc three inches in diameter and a half inch thick and handed it to Chloe. "It amplifies the signals to the meter."

Chloe fingered the cross design etched on one side. "It looks like a medallion," she noted.

Hank reassembled the three blocks in their clear plastic cover, fitted it next to the electronics segment, and replaced the turquoise hood over the entire set. He pressed a button on his desk and walked over to where a large seascape painting slid back to reveal a see-through mirrored panel that overlooked an assembly line. He beckoned to Chloe.

"All the components are connected here at our factory and then sealed completely weather proof and ready to go. Once sealed, there's no need to open them again."

[37]

A well-groomed red-haired man leaned forward and extended his hand as Kevin ducked into the small black limousine. Its plush seats were of beige brushed leather. "Welcome to Los Angeles, Mr. Varyte. I'm Alec LaRose, chief Intel operations officer for Southern Cal, well the whole west coast actually. How was your flight?"

Kevin shook hands firmly. "Alec, pleased to meet you. It was long, but quite comfortable, thanks, just a little bumpy over the Rockies, but not too bad." The elegant vehicle purred into the morning traffic.

"Lindsey Merric filled me in on the case history to date. There isn't much to go on, and we certainly haven't a lot of information beyond what you already know, I'm afraid. This Ashley girl flew in earlier this week. Langley notified us just in time to tag onto her trail. She was picked up here and driven north to a place near Ventura, a mansion-complex up in the hills owned by a Hank Bellard."

LaRose opened a sideboard panel. "Coffee?" he asked.

Kevin raised an eyebrow. "Please," he replied gratefully.

"Cream, sugar?" A steaming thermos rattled in its holder.

"Just a little cream, thanks"

Alec poured two cups and continued. "We've had this place under routine surveillance for a number of years, mainly due to the owner, Hank Bellard. Miss Ashley came through here on the same journey last spring. London notified us that she was a target of interest and traveling into our territory."

"And so, our paths cross," Kevin observed. "Coincidence?"

"More than that, I would guess," LaRose answered. He took a document from his leather briefcase and thumbed through the pages. "Hank Bellard's an old friend; retired from the international oilfield, exploration executive, mechanical and electrical technician, explosives expert for geological tests and for extinguishing well head fires. A lot of these guys know a little bit about everything, it seems. Too bad we can't pay them enough to join our side," he added wryly.

"He's a Texan originally from the Houston area; Vietnam vet, lied about his age to get enlisted, Special Forces, twice wounded, twice decorated, but was later convicted of international activities contrary to national security, 1979. There were a number of earlier offenses; gun running into Mexico, as a kid no less, 1966, got off on a technicality; light arms sales to Palestinian militants in the Jordan, 1968; some shady deals with Saddam's Iraq in the mid 70's. He's no stranger to us. He finally slipped up in Iran making arms deals with remnants of the Tudeh party, which was outlawed by Shahanshah Mohammad Reza Pahlavi for a previous assassination attempt. That basically meant he was working against American foreign policy. You see, the Iranian "King of Kings" was busy buying billions of dollars of our weapons at the time. We couldn't tolerate any operators who could cause business to be siphoned off to the Russians. He was apprehended sometime in the 80s at Tehran boarding a plane to Afghanistan and was deported directly back to the States, where he was sentenced to ten years, and out in five. He was a model prisoner right down the line, spent his time in the gym and the library, and even did a few research papers that were published in government journals, petro-chemical stuff."

Kevin contemplated the man, Bellard. "Quite an interesting fellow. Is he considered dangerous?"

"He is potentially, of course, but there's no indication to what degree, if at all. So that's why we've kept an eye on him," LaRose answered. "He turned up in Cairo for awhile," he consulted his papers, "and then again in Amman and Beirut before fading mostly out of significance for over ten years. He intermittently surfaced in such places as, Dubai, Mumbai, and Sri Lanka, all on what appeared to be legitimate business ventures. Then in 2007, his name was red tagged on the computer here at LAX. It was his first trip back to US soil in some eleven years, plenty of money, sets himself up like a minor king at this place outside Ventura, and by 2012 has established a research type company on the premises. It's called ChemSearch, kind of a catch all name. He had a visit from Xandrieu Xenox earlier this year."

"Xenox?" Kevin queried.

The limousine accelerated with a jerk to avoid being hemmed in by two semi-trucks battling for an outside lane. The coffee swirled over Alec's cup. "Hey, take it easy Chuck," he called into the intercom. "Shit."

"Sorry," a voice answered from behind the smoky bullet proof glass partition. "Traffic."

He returned his attention to Kevin, "Now where the hell was I?"

"Xenox," Kevin replied.

"Right, another friend from way back, this one's a Greek immigrant, an export-import shipping tycoon in New York City." He flipped open a separate folder. "Came up the hard way, with all that that implies. He's behind a lot of Middle Eastern connections, the usual, Yemen, Lebanon, Libya, no dealings with Israel, a confirmed Palestinian sympathizer, no surprises there. He is well known for ruthlessness. We have documented a number of cases where his enemies disappeared in accidents, some of them explosions. Nothing provable, and in some cases he was doing us a favor, so let's say, we didn't pursue evidence collection very aggressively. As far as the law is concerned, he's clean."

"Two gems in one setting," Kevin added.

"Exactly, so we've stepped our observations up a smidge and now this Ashley gal shows up as well. All we've learned is that Bellard's ChemSearch has had a significant increase in activity over the last several months. A steady stream of electronic devices has been coming in from China, along with various other components from other countries, via the Mediterranean, Pakistan for instance. We haven't made much sense out of it yet, but we were able to turn one of his employees sometime ago, a fellow named Dean, driver and gofer, has a family to support. We give him an income supplement, and he gives us information. He'll try to get ahold of one of these electronic gizmos that Bellard's assembling up there."

[38]

Dean stood in the dusty hard baked court yard under the early afternoon sun. This late in the year it was comfortably warm but no longer sweltering. He had parked his ChemSearch van strategically behind Hank Bellard's warehouse where it blocked the general view of a stack of crates that had recently been delivered to the premises. He glanced around to make sure the area was deserted, then carefully pried open the closest crate with a large screwdriver. He pulled out one of the turquoise blue plastic boxes. The invoice read that the merchandise had been assembled in China. "Big surprise," he said to himself.

It was fairly light weight. He hastily rearranged the stuffing material so it would appear that the crate had been packed with one box short, and tapped the lid shut. He slipped the one he held into the van, covered it with an oily cloth and slid the door shut. Out of the corner of his eye, Dean was startled to see a young man climb over the high back wall. He crouched immediately out of sight, alert. The young man was an obvious foreigner, but Dean couldn't guess from where.

Ahmed dropped to the ground and ran quickly into the shadows of the warehouse and worked his way warily around a jumble of machinery parts towards a side door. He picked up a piece of pipe and tried to pry the padlock loose, but it wouldn't budge. Dean chose the moment to intervene. He shuffled soundlessly from behind the van and grabbed Ahmed from behind with both arms. The young Egyptian struggled with desperation but was easily subdued by the larger American.

"Alright you rascal," Dean exclaimed. "Just what the devil do you think you're up to?"

Ahmed momentarily thrashed in panic like a banked fish but quickly resigned himself to his fate. He was caught. "Let me go," he whined.

"Right," Dean answered firmly twisting the youth's arms behind his back. "In a minute or two, but first we'll make a little trip to see the boss. This way." He pushed Ahmed along the courtyard to the main entrance of the warehouse, and backed him through the metal doors. Hank Bellard looked up from his discussion with Sam, his assembly line foreman. Dean dragged Ahmed over to them. "I caught this scalawag trying to break into the warehouse," he explained to their curious expressions.

Bellard stared at Ahmed a long moment. "Ma ismuka?" he asked harshly.

"Ahmed," the young Egyptian responded before gasping. He had already been tricked.

"So, you're an Arab," Hank replied. Ahmed nodded. "And you are from …?"

"Egypt, I am from Egypt," Ahmed answered weakly.

Hank rubbed his chin. "Egypt?" he mused in a more forgiving tone. "You're a long way from home, aren't you?"

"I … uh … my wife and I … uh … we live in Ventura … I … work in a restaurant," Ahmed stuttered.

"Is this a restaurant?" Hank asked waving an arm impatiently. Ahmed shook his head. "Well, then what the hell are you doing breaking in here?"

Ahmed quivered slightly, "I ... uh ... I heard that perhaps there was a job," he blurted out convincingly. He had rehearsed his cover story but had just remembered to use it.

Dean leaned close to Ahmed's frightened face. "You do have front doors in Egypt, don't you?"

Ahmed felt himself gaining credibility. He thought fast. "I ... I wanted to find out more, what kind of job." He half believed it himself. "I thought because I am Egyptian ..." he let the sentence trail off.

Bellard looked at Sam and Dean and laughed heartily. "Well, Ahmed. I like your spirit," he snorted. "Your style, I can do without." He turned to the line supervisor, "Well, Sam what do you think?"

Sam ran a hand through his hair and scratched his scalp. "Well, if you put it that way, I suppose we could always use another set of hands on the assembly line. It's not difficult work or difficult to learn, and we have increased our product completion rate these last weeks. Orders are steady, what the hell, why not?"

"Fine," Hank chuckled, "This reminds me of how I got my first oil rig job." He laughed again. "Come up in the morning, then. Sam here will show you the ropes. No more snooping and learn to use the front door, eh?" He swatted Ahmed on the shoulder. "Sam, stop by my office around five," he said and exited up a stairway and through a door that led directly to his office.

Sam looked over the scruffy Egyptian and moaned. "Well, you heard the man," he said. "Be here at eight, on the nose, Abdul."

"Ahmed," Ahmed said.

"Eight o'clock, Abdul," Sam repeated as Dean led the young man back out to the warehouse courtyard.

- - -

Ahmed sat subdued next to Dean as the van twisted down the dirt road from the foothills. Dean pulled the van over and stopped by a large scrub bush. He grinned with a touch of embarrassment, "Just a second, here." He switched the engine off, pocketed the key and disappeared behind the brush. Ahmed could hear the man relieving himself.

He ventured a look around the inside of the vehicle and saw a bundle covered with oil-stained cloth shoved behind the driver's seat. He reached cautiously back and lifted the cloth exposing a tough plastic bluish box. There was some kind of glass meter dial on top. He tapped it and the needle squiggled. Ahmed hastily dropped the messy rag when he heard Dean returning.

"Ah," Dean sighed. "That's much better," he said climbing back behind the wheel and firing up the engine. He whistled a little as the van continued its roll down the deserted road towards sea level. "I gotta say this for you, Ahmed, you certainly got balls. No brains, that's for sure."

Ahmed remained silent.

(39)

Kevin reclined on the beige brushed leather sofa in Alec LaRose's lower Sunset Boulevard office. He gazed thoughtfully at the large world wall map over his head. He mentally traced his surveillance of the girl; London, Paris, Malta, Libya and now these months later, California. The golden apparition he had seen that night at the Saharan oasis warehouse was here.

"I wonder why?" he said absently out loud.

"What?" Alec asked lifting his head from his paperwork.

"Oh, nothing. I was just thinking ..." Kevin began when the door opened and a man entered carrying a bundle wrapped in oily cloth. He walked to the desk and plunked it solidly down in front of Alec.

"For Christ's sake, Dean. Get this shit off my desk," Alec complained.

"Evening, Alec," Dean said removing the cloth with all the extravagance of a sculptor unveiling his latest creation. The cloth left extravagant oil smears on the desk, as well.

"Son of a bitch! Look at this mess." The chief rubbed the desk top with tissue.

Unconcerned, Dean continued. "Well, as you can see, I managed to get one." Kevin stood up and walked over for a closer look. Dean gave a surprised start.

"Dean," Alec said. "This is Kevin Varyte, from our guys in Washington, via London."

"Oh, hi. I didn't know anyone else was here," Dean replied with embarrassment. They shook hands.

"So, this is what the Bellard commotion is all about," LaRose said turning his attention back to the plastic box on his desk. "What is it?"

"Some kind of a meter?" Kevin asked.

"It seems so," Dean answered. "I'll find out more in a few days." He removed the meter hood to uncover the electronic mechanism and chip card package which was hard wired to the bottom section. There was a large empty slot next to that. He pointed out the components as best he could, the meter, the loose wires and the electronics. "I've only been able to gather general information about these devices, so far," he apologized.

Alec prompted him. "What is the vacant space there?" he asked indicating an obviously missing major component.

"I'm not sure exactly. I only got a glimpse of some plans in the warehouse, some kind of vibration sensitive material and, I think, maybe a battery. He stepped over to a bookshelf and selected several moderately sized books. "Like this," he said and slid two of the thicker books into the slot and demonstrated where the loose electrical wires might connect the rest of the instrument to a power source. "It would power the whole dang thing, I suppose," he concluded.

"And the girl?" Kevin asked.

"She's been here all week conferring with Bellard; it seems mainly about distribution of these contraptions throughout the country. Which reminds me," Dean said looking at his watch. "She's returning to New York on the red eye. I've gotta pick her up in a couple of hours, take her to LAX."

(40)

Lindsey, Sheldon, Scott and Gloria sat together again abstractly staring, or rather, avoiding staring, at each, other across the same mahogany conference table. On one side, a technician stood patiently. On the table before him were a computer with its flat screen console and the turquoise box that Dean had "borrowed" from the ChemSearch warehouse in Ventura two months earlier. The hood was removed, laid separately on the table with the meter and solar cell panel facing up. It was now connected by extended wires to the internal mechanisms of the base. On a green chalk board, the technician had drawn a diagram for further clarity.

Lindsey glanced at his gold Rolex with irritation. The others behaved with suitable discomfort to match their chief's mood. Gloria fiddled with her pen. Scott cleaned his spectacles. Sheldon changed flints in his gas lighter. The technician gazed out the window and rearranged already rearranged wires. Footsteps sounded in the hall. Kevin opened the door and strode confidently in. With a flourish of wetness, he removed his raincoat and hung it on the rack to drip dry.

"Right on time, as usual," Lindsey commented sarcastically.

Kevin sat himself next to Gloria and looked at the group innocently and held up his hands. "Traffic," he said half apologetically and half mockingly. "When it rains, the cars just pile up out there." He nodded to the case officers for the Levant and North Africa. "Sheldon, Scott, good to see you." With a wink, he added, "Gloria, always good to see you." Gloria blushed and smiled warmly. Kevin folded his hands as in prayer and turned to the boss. "Lindsey, it's always a pleasure," he drawled. "I see life at the top hasn't changed much in my absence."

Lindsey glared back. "Some things never change."

"I've noticed," Kevin replied with ill disguised resignation.

Sensing the growing embarrassment, the technician cleared his throat. "If this is everyone, I may as well begin," he said. It was enough to dissipate the tension. Lindsey gave him the go ahead with a nod. "Well, the lab boys took this device apart down to the last electronic board which wasn't difficult. It's pretty simple and straightforward. They didn't need to remove any chips or anything unnecessary like that. Then they reassembled it and connected it up as you see it now. It is a sophisticated type of stress and vibration monitor. Very well constructed and they used the best materials available."

He went on to explain the different components of the unit referring to his chalk diagram and to the device itself. "It had a setting for a ten-ton minimum level when we got it ..."

"Which means?" Kevin interrupted.

"Which means," the technician continued. "That anything less than ten tons in weight will not register on either the meter or the recorder."

"Which, we believe, would narrow its range down to monitoring heavy traffic" Lindsey added. "This opens endless avenues of speculation, military espionage for one thing."

"Exactly," the engineering tech stated. "But it is so easily recalibrated that it could have multiple uses. We adjusted it for laboratory testing." He waved a data downloading wand similar to one used by electricity meter readers close to the electronics package. "We got this from the Potomac Electric Power Company," he chortled. "And I just collected the results from right here in this room."

"You mean this thing's been recording?" Sheldon asked.

The technician simply downloaded the wand into a device connected to the computer and dimmed the overhead lights. "We rigged up this playback system which will be similar to what they will have to use." The screen lit up with a pale green glow. A brighter green line dissected the screen. As it began to oscillate, a paper graph simultaneously printed a data line graph. "Here is where Mr. Merric, the two gentlemen and the lady entered the room and sat down." The line smoothed out with only occasional blips. He briefly pressed a fast forward button. The group waited patiently. The line again flickered and became wrinkled again. "And this is Mr. Varyte entering."

With the demonstration concluded, the technician raised the lights and tore the printed graph from the computer. He handed it to Gloria to pass around. "We got the whole package except for what we must suppose are the battery and some kind of vibration detection material. We approximated what they might be and incorporated them into our experiments. If it wasn't necessary for the instrument to be portable, you could even hook the entire unit up to a wall socket, with a step-down transformer, naturally."

"Naturally," Kevin said.

"All in all, it seems to be an excellent vibration measuring tool for materials stress management," the tech concluded.

Lindsey took control, "Thank you, Thomas, and if there are no further questions?" He looked at the others. All shook their heads. He waved the technician away and the man exited leaving the equipment on the table. "So, there you have it. It appears to be a straight forward scientific product, one of about two or three thousand per week that ChemSearch is assembling in California."

Scott reached for his credit card sized calculator. Tap, tap, tap. "That's about three hundred and fifty to five hundred per day, assuming a six-day week, no mechanical problems. And an eight-hour day, would be forty to sixty an hour. That's quite an operation," he said rolling his eyes.

"Correct," Lindsey agreed. "But LaRose in LA reports there are two shifts keeping the factory going about 16 hours, every day except Sunday. So, those figures become more manageable, say, up to thirty an hour. And if it weren't for the illustrious people involved, Xenox and Bellard, I would have to say it is a perfectly legitimate business, even an economy booster."

"And we all know that needs some stimulating," Scott observed.

"But who are they for?" Kevin asked.

"StresChek," Sheldon told him.

"Excuse me?"

"It seems to be the name of the operating company. ChemSearch is the supplier; StresChek is the receiver, the installer and the operator. They are using the devices to measure stresses on freeway over pass supports, train bridges and other similar structures."

"We easily traced the first shipments to Chicago and New York," Lindsey continued. "They were received by StresChek offices in both cities, all located in business park offices with industrial storage and warehouse access, truck ports and the like. There are small fleets of service vans and tech drivers that go out and attach the devices onto the cement columns with steel bands. They've been mostly doing test readings so far, so they've been returning twice a week or so to download data. That will later be reduced to a monthly check."

Kevin gave a questioning look, "How...?"

Sheldon answered it. "Some of their technicians are ours."

"Of course," Kevin nodded.

"The connection with Xenox goes way up to high levels on the Hill," Gloria added. "A traffic safety bill was tacked onto the latest Stimulus Package for, what else? National security concerns. City government councils across the country were allocated funds earmarked for these stress tests, use 'em or lose 'em type programs. Promote responsible domestic energy resource development and the construction of transportation infrastructure through activism and strategies for change. That type of thing. Xenox had some powerful lobbyists influencing the bill. These traffic improvement projects always sound good on paper, whether they're needed or not, and rake in the votes, so local politicians love to be associated with them."

"And since Xenox's own StresChek is the only company in the business and already primed to go, he scooped up all the contracts with no competition," Lindsey emphasized.

"Exclusive and no-bid before any potential rival even knew it was happening," Gloria added.

"As a matter of fact," Scott spoke. "The contracts had already been sewn up months before the laws were even passed. The cities just waited for the stimulus allocations to go into effect to make the deals legit. Xenox stands to make billions, and the cities rake in funds, get elaborate tax breaks and financial shelters on top of it all. Not to mention voter satisfaction for reelection bids."

Kevin whistled softly.

"Yes, Kevin," Lindsey said. "That was our conclusion, too."

Kevin ignored the patronizing. "So, this might not be connected to Sparrow's trips for the Xenox Corporation to the Middle East which even if they are suspicious could be legit as well?" he asked.

"Perhaps," Lindsey admitted. "There are indications that there are some components that might be related to these devices coming out of the area, but we haven't anything concrete to go on."

"So?" Kevin nudged.

"So, we need to keep tabs on her nonetheless," Lindsey continued. "Just to be sure, and to cover our own hinders if something undue does occur. And in the meantime, there's not much we can do about Bellard's ChemSearch or Xenox's StresChek partnership, except sit tight, assess the situation and keep everything under at least a minimal surveillance. They've got all their bases covered."

A silence followed that even Kevin was reluctant to break.

"Comments?" Lindsey eventually asked. There were none. "Alright, then case closed for now. There are more serious matters of concern worldwide than this little sideshow." The group rose to leave, all but Lindsey who sat pondering. He let Kevin get halfway through the door before stopping him. "One moment, Kevin," he called.

Kevin stood holding his raincoat in the doorway. "Sir?"

"Oh, I'm sending you to Cairo. Sparrow has returned to her old route again. I want you available in the area, just in case, for a while longer. Check with Gloria, on Monday, would you?"

Kevin winced, there were better places to be in winter than Egypt, he envisioned a nip off to somewhere less troubled, but he smiled cheerfully. "Thank you, sir."

[41]

Ahmed found that adjusting to the StresChek assembly line was easier than he had imagined. He worried over it the first night with Fatima after they had moved up to Ventura, but after a few days, several minor mistakes and a couple of severe reprimands from the foreman, Ahmed had fully adapted to the routine. Now as the days dragged on into weeks, and the weeks to months, his main concern was becoming "Why am I here?"

Reaching across to a near table, he picked up one of the completed detection battery packs that had been stacked there for his station. He liked the clear covering and being able to see the inside components for a change, the green, the red and the blue, all washed out pale colors. Three blocks incased in clear plastic with electrical terminals on top. Sam had pointed out their functions. "The green detects vibrations, the red is an insulator, and the blue is a solar charged battery. Just double check that they are in the right order before you install them. If you find a defect, we'll just send it back"

He placed the package in its space in the base of the turquoise box, next to the electronics, and reached for his solder gun. His mind drifted back to his original purpose for coming to California. He despairingly asked himself, "What more can I accomplish here? I found the place where the shipment from Athens was being sent to when father was killed. Now what? Maybe Fatima is right. Maybe it is hopeless. What if it is just me trying to link two incidents together? What if they are not related at all?"

He tested his connections for tightness and then with an oscilloscope. The lighted bleeps in complete sine waves showed the connections were secure and conducting. He set the unit on a slow-moving conveyor belt and watched as it moved to the next station where an older guy connected the remaining wires to the meter and solar panel and placed the outer hood over the whole works. After he tested his connections, another man placed the completed box in a heat press and pulled a lever.

The plastic edges sizzled under intense heat and pressure. The press lever was released after fifteen to twenty seconds with a sigh of steam, and the unit was permanently and tightly sealed and stamped with a StresChek logo melted onto the side. The finished products were neatly stacked on wooden pallets, covered in a wrap, and removed by forklift for immediate shipping by continuously arriving and departing trucks.

It was a smooth-running operation and the foreman, Sam, was proud of it, and therefore, demanding of his subordinates.

Ahmed didn't mind. He was making wages he could only dream about in Egypt. Perhaps in Dubai and some of the other Emirates there was such work, but from what he had heard, the living conditions there were atrocious and dangerous for immigrant labor. In comparison, the daily routine of his work life in America was seductive and appealing without a doubt.

"I must concentrate on father's murderers," he angrily reminded himself, again. When break time came around, he walked over to a soda machine, deposited a couple of dollar bills and punched Root Beer. What a novelty, he thought, returning to his station. He had never heard of it before, nor had many others outside of North America. He sat in mild frustration on his swivel chair and took a long sip of the cool beverage. At the far end of the warehouse, at the top of the metal stairway that ascended up to the entrance to Bellard's office, a door opened. Sam, the foreman came out onto the platform and held the door for Hank who was showing a visitor around the premises.

Ahmed gasped with the shock of recognition, then doubt, followed by certainty. He choked on his soda. His neighbor worker gave him a curious look, but Ahmed had his full attention focused on the visitor across the floor. He felt triumph and defeat well up together making his chest nearly burst.

"Xenox," he whispered furiously. The trio at the far end glanced briefly around while Sam gestured at the machinery and conveyor belts, and then departed back through the same door. Ahmed was left staring blankly at the empty spot. A plump fellow wheeled a full cart of battery packages towards Ahmed's work station and hefted another two dozen onto his work table.

"Delivery for one Mr. Ahab," he announced jovially. Ahab the Arab he called his new Middle Eastern friend.

"What? Yeah, okay," Ahmed replied with a faraway glare.

"Hey, are you okay? You look like you've just seen a ghost."

"Maybe I have," Ahmed said in a low stammer. He turned back to his work with a sullen scowl.

The stout worker shrugged and went his way. Foreigners, he thought, who can figure them?

[42]

Fatima opened the balcony door of their small apartment overlooking the dark Pacific Ocean. The moon was disappearing over the horizon. "But how can you be sure?" she demanded.

"I tell you," Ahmed asserted. "I know that man, that face. My father showed me a photograph of him one night when I was little. My father was in the picture also. He told me, 'See this man, Ahmed. He is a type, a special type of man. The world has always had them and it always will. You must beware; beware of this kind of man. They will make you wonder if you are human or just an animal.' He was drinking, my father, and I'm sure he never thought I would remember. But I have never forgotten."

Fatima stepped into the cool night. The moon was gone. Ahmed joined his new wife on the tiny terrace. She was attempting to hold back tears. "I don't like this," she sniffled.

(43)

A blue and white Ford lunch van pulled in through the back gates and stopped with a screech of rusty brake pads. The ChemSearch employees filed into the courtyard and lined up as the blond woman in blue denim jeans and checked shirt climbed in back to open up the sales window and stock the Formica counter with plastic wrapped sandwiches and bags of snacks. Dean had just moved to the front of the queue when Ahmed put down his work and came outside.

"Hey Dean," he called as soon as he saw the driver. Dean came over with a ham and cheese on rye in one hand and a pint orange juice carton in the other.

"Hey, hi, kiddo. How's it going?" Dean said. "Haven't seen you in a few days. I've been a bit busy with all these shipments coming and going. What's up?"

"That fat man that was here yesterday, who is he?" Ahmed asked.

"Fat man? Oh, you mean Xenox?" Dean guessed.

The Egyptian narrowed his eyes and answered slowly. "Yeah, Xenox. Who is he?"

Dean munched on his sandwich and took a swig of orange juice. "Oh, just one of Bellard's partners, does some financing, too, I guess."

"Where does he come from?" Ahmed demanded roughly.

"New York," Dean replied annoyed. "Hey, Ahmed, what's with all the questions all of a sudden? You've been pretty quiet up 'til now, you know."

"What does he do?" Ahmed continued unabated.

"Look, I told you. He's a financial partner of Hank's."

"I mean, who does he work for?" Ahmed pressed.

"Ahmed, forget Xenox," Dean answered impatiently. "It's none of your business, anyway."

The Egyptian squared off with the driver and glared into his eyes. "Well, I'm making it my business," he hissed.

Dean angrily elbowed him back. "Look, Ahmed, you wanna live long in this world? Then you mind your own business, lesson number one. Got it?"

"Like you mind your own business?" Ahmed said cynically, prompting the desired reaction from Dean.

He was angry now and grabbed the young man by the collar and pulled him aside. "What's that supposed to mean?" he fumed.

"I've seen you around here," Ahmed answered flatly. "No one else notices, but I see you snooping around, looking at papers and files. Why is a driver so nosey?" He allowed himself to get cocky. "Tell me, what did you do with the vibration meter box you stole the day you caught me trying to break in the warehouse?"

"Mind your own friggin' business," he growled bristling. Then, sensing more, he calmed down and looked closely at Ahmed. "What's your interest in this anyway?" he asked.

Ahmed answered stonily. "That man, Xenox, I think he killed my father."

Dean slowly released his grip on Ahmed's shirt.

(44)

The sun dipped below the Pacific waters casting glimmering slivers of gold across its broken surface. Waves slogged through thick kelp paddies along the shore and fell with wallops onto the coarse sand. The air was not yet disturbed by the coolness of evening. Dean reached down and picked up a small spiny shell at his feet.

"I was in Greece to help with my father's export import business. He was very busy in Cairo, and wanted me to learn the practices of operations," Ahmed explained. "My father was killed by a bomb in the Cairo central souk. It had something to do with the shipment, I'm sure of it. My father never sent me before." He sighed, thinking back to happier days. "There were crates there at the Piraeus docks waiting to be loaded onto a container ship. The boxes were destined for California, to ChemSearch. I came looking for answers."

"And what was in these crates that makes you so sure they had anything to do with your dad's death?" Dean asked. "It seems like a pretty flimsy connection there."

"I don't know, tourist medallions, I guess," Ahmed answered.

"Medallions, you say?" Dean searched his memory. "Round and a little heavy, about a half inch thick? Maybe three inches in diameter?"

"Yes," Ahmed answered bitterly. "There were thousands of them from somewhere in India, I think. Father always did a lot of bulk souvenir purchasing, I know."

"And these medallion things were slivery, but not really precious, with a funny cross like design on one side?"

"Yes, the one I saw had an intricate cross carving. How did you know?"

Dean thought back to the shipment at the Port. "I cleared a load of them myself some months ago, at San Pedro. They came in at the Foreign Trade Zone, nice gal, I recall, stamped the paper work. And that's right; they were from Greece now that you mention it. Most of the Port's traffic comes from the Asian side, so it was a little unusual. I didn't give it much thought at the time. I just did the paper work, cleared them into the US and brought the invoices up to Hank. Someone else picked them up. I haven't seen any sign of them up at the factory now that you mention it. Now I wish I'd kept one."

- - -

Further south, dusk fell quickly. The golden hues of sunset sank into hazy reds, unusual lavenders, and finally dissolved into a tranquil indigo night. The greater Los Angeles lowlands with its endless rows of sodium lights glowed under its close smoggy atmosphere. The freeway arteries of the city sparkled and flowed like lava. Near the entrance to the Los Angeles International Port, in a new Port City manufacturing facility conveniently located for port related enterprises, fluorescent lights flared inside a warehouse alive with activity. Operations had just recently been set in motion with the help of special government stimulus funds. The Port Authority was grateful for the business, and the work force was happy for the much-needed employment. Twelve short assembly lines were busily at work. All the workers wore similar aprons, protective breathing masks and white opaque latex gloves. The scene resembled a discount surgery hospital, if any such place existed.

A set of hands lifted one pale red plastic block, eight by six by two inches, from a box of many, and set it on its side on a work counter. A circular recess was exposed about three inches in diameter. The hands then picked out a single small metal disc from another box and inserted it into the special recess. It fit perfectly flat with the surface. The technician made sure that the unusual cross design etched on the disc faced outwards per assembly instructions. She then reached for another equal sized pale green block and placed it on the left side of the red one with the metal disc still visible. The last block was blue of a similar pale hue and placed on the right. It covered the metal disc. All three were each coated in a stiff paraffin wax. Holding the three blocks as one, she slid them to her neighbor worker who placed them on a special rotating table, looped a tough black thread around them and pressed a foot pedal switch. The spinning wheel unwound a specific length of twine around the blocks securely binding them snugly together, then automatically snipped the end off.

This job done, the colorful package was passed on to the next worker who hastily snatched it up and worked it into a clear hard plastic casing box. Next, a cap was tapped with a rubber hammer onto the top until a snap signaled it was properly closed. The clear cap had two electrical terminals on top, and inside three copper spikes penetrated each of the green, red and blue paraffin blocks. This unit was sent down an inclined roller counter to another set of eager hands that painted a chemically melding silicon sealer around the cap top seam and placed the completed battery pack into a shipping crate. The destination on the crate was stamped, ChemSearch Production Facilities. The contents label read, Three Phase Battery Units, 36 quantity per box. The shipping symbols warned of electrical and hazardous materials inside.

- - -

Dean steered Ahmed onto a long pier that stretched over the Pacific shoreline and into the darkness. "So, what about you? What is your story?" Ahmed asked.

Dean stopped to lean on the railing and drop his spiny shell into the water below. "Let's just say I'm with the authorities," Dean replied.

"Okay, the authorities," Ahmed nodded. "And now what are you going to do?"

"Do?" Dean questioned, peering down at a school of small silvery fish that dove for the shell.

"Yes, do!" Ahmed tried not to shout. "He's a criminal. He murdered or had my father murdered!"

"And at least a dozen others, that I've been told about," Dean commented offhandedly. He kicked a bottle cap into the water to see the fish dive again.

"Damn it, then why don't you arrest him?"

"Sorry, Ahmed. It doesn't work that way. Not here in America," he said holding his palms up. "There's no evidence. He'd get off on any of a hundred technicalities." He kicked a flattened soda can towards a trash basket under one of the pole lights lining the pier. "Guys like Xenox keep themselves legally clean no matter how dirty they may be. All we can do is wait."

"Wait?" Ahmed said incredulously. 'Wait?"

"And watch. That's what I'm doing, watching. If something's amiss up there," he gestured behind him towards the dark foothills, "I'll find out. I'd hate to see that happen, though. Old Bellard's a pretty nice guy, as things go. I'm not overly fond of some of his associates, Xenox for one, but that's a different story altogether. Anyway, if something's not kosher, no offence," he added wryly, "someone will slip up. They always do."

"Always?" Ahmed asked skeptically.

"Usually," Dean shrugged.

"Usually?" Ahmed stared at the man with an expression of utter disbelief.

"Well, okay, sometimes," Dean admitted.

(45)

Kevin bent forward and pushed a bright red tee into the scrubby grass at his feet and balanced a clean white ball on top. He stood straight, flexed his fingers and chose a number, whatever, club from a teenage caddy who stood several feet away in a traditional Arab outfit. He didn't know the club numbers, but figured the biggest one had to be the best for the first shot. Kevin glanced over to a garden table where a group of secretaries and minor embassy officials sniggered. He tapped the club on the ground and gazed purposefully into the distance. He took his most professional looking swing, but that was all it was, professional looking.

The club cracked solidly sending the ball sailing straight over the low palm bushes on his right. The ball hit hard against a mud brick boundary wall with a dead thud and fell behind a tangle of oleanders. "Damn!" Kevin cursed.

The snickers at the table erupted. "Hey that was great," someone shouted.

"Nice shot," one of the girls called.

Kevin returned to the table and sat with and in a huff. This Cairo trip wasn't working out at all. The laughter gradually subsided. An attendant came over to the group and was trying to get anyone's attention.

"Mr. Varyte?" he asked, in between the outbursts of mirth that had the group self absorbed.

"Hey, Kevin, dear. Someone has a message for you."

"I know maybe it's the PGA. They want him to play professionally."

"Look out Myrtle Beach!" Wally Kitterman, the chief liaison officer, laughed

"More like, McMurdo beach, he can represent Antarctica." The laughter reached a crescendo.

The attendant called Kevin to the telephone. Amid a chorus of hoots and giggles, he stood up, bowed and walked to the clubhouse. The golf course was conveniently situated on a Nile island in central Cairo. Kevin had an unobstructed view of buildings from the bar where the club telephone was situated. "Kevin Varyte," he said.

"Kevin, they want you to intercept Sparrow in flight at Frankfurt tomorrow. Your papers and tickets are being finalized as we speak." It was the voice of the junior officer from the London Embassy.

[46]

At Frankfurt Terminal 1, Kevin waited patiently by a dark window. In the reflection, he studied the line of passengers waiting to board the Lufthansa Air Bus A320 flight LH3518 for Beirut, Lebanon. This was a nice choice of flight, leaving after nine at night and arriving in the Middle East in the wee hours of morning, Kevin thought. "Charming," he said to himself. There were other flights at more reasonable hours. Middle East Airlines Air Liban, for one, had an early afternoon choice, but Sparrow had always traveled on this night flight for some reason.

He had arrived early, some hours ago, so as to be ahead of the blonde woman he was to make contact with. She would be transiting off a Swiss International Airlines flight from Zurich. She might not make the flight on time, he reminded himself. So many variables came into play with air travel, but the chances were, she would. Still, when the ticket counter woman announced boarding for the second time, he was uncomfortable. Chloe was nowhere in sight.

He watched the line grow smaller as the passengers showed their tickets and passports and disappeared through the boarding ramp door. A hand tapped him on the shoulder, "Sir?" a voice asked, "Are you on this flight?" He turned around. A Lufthansa hostess looked at him questioningly.

Kevin nodded, "To Beirut, yes."

She indicated towards the check-in counter, "We are boarding now."

"Yes," he explained, "Sorry, I was just waiting." He was the last passenger in the lounge. He didn't much care for the idea of a wasted journey, but he knew he'd be unable to avoid boarding the plane at the last minute. If Chloe was a no show, he would still have to go through the motions of his cover. There was just too much confusion and miscommunication amongst the European authorities these days to risk arousing undue suspicion by trying to exit a flight at the last minute, especially on a trip to Beirut. He showed the woman his passport and ticket and walked with her to the ramp.

He strode down the metal passageway to the airplane door. High octane fumes and engine whines filtered in from the darkness outside. The flight stewardess checked his ticket one last time and led him to his First-Class seat. The plane was nowhere near full. He took the outside seat. "Not a full flight tonight?" He said trying to keep his spirits up. The stewardess agreed.

He placed his carry-on under his seat. The cabin door was closed and the catering area clattered with the noise of the preflight routine. Kevin had just sat back with weary resignation when the cabin door was jolted open. Another passenger came through the doorway. Kevin was relieved to catch a glimpse of flowing blonde hair. She came through the curtain, out of breath and took the seat two rows in front of Kevin. Kevin closed his eyes with relief and relaxed.

A half hour later as the plane climbed to cruising altitude and the seat belt lights turned off, Kevin stood up in the aisle and stretched. He opened the overhead rack forward of his seat and carefully pulled out a blanket allowing a pillow to fall further forward. His aim was perfect. The small pillow fell onto Chloe's lap just brushing her hair.

Kevin leaned over apologetically. "Oh, excuse me. How clumsy of me. I'm so sorry."

The girl looked up and handed the handsome gentleman his pillow. Kevin allowed their eyes to make contact. He melted involuntarily with a sheepish grin. "No bother," she said returning his smile.

"What takes you to Beirut?" he asked to avoid sitting down.

"Me?" she answered as if just waking up to her own presence. "Oh, I work for Inter-Swiss, the consulting firm, financial officer type, nothing too exciting. I'm usually out here every other week for something or other."

"But very interesting, I'm sure" Kevin commented.

"Not really," she answered. "But it does keep me traveling and paying the bills."

"I know what you mean," Kevin said sympathetically. "I get out to Lebanon maybe twice a year, myself." A stewardess came through with a dinner cart. Kevin stepped aside and took an empty seat across the aisle. "I'm into gold and silver, mostly for industrial purposes," he said continuing the conversation. "Were you in Frankfurt long?"

"No, my flight in from Zurich on Swiss was delayed by weather. I nearly didn't make the connection."

"I noticed," Kevin said. "They had already closed the door." He changed the subject. "Ah, Switzerland, my favorite country," he sighed. "Are you Swiss, then?"

"No, just English, I'm afraid" she replied apologetically as if admitting to a perceived crime.

"Well, nobody is perfect," Kevin said with a wink. "I'm an American, for instance. But I do work out of London," he added as if that somehow made it alright.

"I see what you mean."

"About what?" Kevin asked perplexed.

"About no one being perfect," she answered with a laugh. The stewardess came by with dinner trays. They both asked for the fish and seemed to share a taste for red wine as well. This somehow seemed encouraging to Kevin for some odd reason. Through dinner, they kept up a casual conversation about nothing in particular. Chloe would occasionally laugh about or at something Kevin said. When the trays were cleared, Chloe placed her briefcase on the window seat next to her and apologized that she had some work to catch up on. Kevin nodded understandingly and rose to return to his assigned seat. "Perhaps, I'll see you later," he said. "Oh, I'm Christopher Josephs, by the way."

"That would be nice," Chloe answered. "I'm Jennifer Newton."

Kevin reclined back in his seat. He enjoyed the darkened cabin, the main saving grace of night flying. He listened as the turbulent miles thundered by, lost in the kind of thoughts he usually didn't permit himself. Two rows ahead of him, haloed under her overhead reading light, sat the apparition he had glimpsed so briefly all those months ago in the deep Sahara. She was far more beautiful close up, he mused.

(47)

The intercom speakers gonged obnoxiously and the cabin lights fluttered back on with a painful glare. Kevin awoke with a start. He had dozed off, another luxury he usually avoided.

"We have started our descent into Beirut International Airport and should be on the ground in twenty minutes," the hostess announced. "The local time is 2 AM. The temperature is 15 Centigrade. There is a cloud layer."

When the plane groaned to a halt, Kevin rose to be near Chloe. "In Beirut for long?" he asked helping her with her carry-on from the overhead bin.

"Maybe a week," she said glancing in her pocket mirror.

"A bit longer than me. Where are you staying?"

"Well, I used to stay at the Hotel Saint George," she answered.

The Saint George, Beirut's premier luxury hotel and its most famous. It was a hot spot of classic Cold War intrigue throughout the 1960's and most recently the tragic scene of the 2005 bomb assassination of Rafik Hariri, the Lebanese President He had put his life and fortune into reconstructing the civil war-torn capital city and was repaid with death. The hotel was now locked in a rebuilding conflict which prevented reconstruction and was still out of business. "After the assassination, I would always book into the Phoenicia, of course. But now, with that insane ammonium nitrate explosion in the port silos, all the old hotels are decimated. I hear the Phoenicia is opening again, but I've changed hotels already."

Kevin shook his head wearily. "This city just can't seem to get enough of destruction and tragedy," he sighed.

"So, now I'm staying at the Hilton Habtoor, not as scenically located but oh well, you have to take what you can get these days."

"What a coincidence," Kevin beamed. "That's where I'm booked. The Hilton hotels are always so convenient," he added. He thought briefly of his reservations at the Movenpick. But, no worries, his chances for getting a room at the Hilton were good in winter. The added pleasure of handing Lindsey a greatly increased expense account made him grin inwardly.

Chloe smiled sweetly, "How nice."

- - -

Kevin caught up with Chloe after passport control and customs. She was waiting with a tow suitcase at the curb in front of the arrivals hall. The night was cool and scented with humidity. "Hi there," Kevin called. "Hey, as long as we're going to the same place, how about sharing a taxi?"

Chloe declined. "Thanks, but I have a car." She smiled as a polished black Mercedes pulled up next to her. A driver rushed out, took her bag and held the door open for her. She waved from the window as the car pulled off towards a pine lined avenue that led into the city. Kevin sighed and hailed a grey taxi, also a Mercedes, but somewhat older and much scruffier. A couple of teenagers sat up front, one driving. A rifle butt protruded from under their seat.

"Hilton Hotel, Charles de Gaulle Street," Kevin said warily.

(48)

Chloe sat blinking in the late morning sunrays. The clouds had all but dissipated. Afar, she could see snow covered Mount Sannin directly to the east, and the many towns and villages creeping up the closer slopes. She sipped a cup of French coffee and gazed across the city. The deep ultramarine waters were distant but visible towards Jounieh Bay. The city had been reconstructed quite elaborately since the civil war but there were many traces of pock marks on walls attesting to the furious fighting that had rocked the city for fifteen years. An uneasiness still lingered.

"Ah, there you are," Kevin said as he walked through the Le Ciel 31st floor dining hall doors. Chloe's face registered a delighted "Oh no, not you" expression. "Sleeping late? Where have you been hiding?" he asked. "I had to have breakfast alone. So not to let that happen again, let me treat you to dinner?"

Chloe laughed with mock exasperation and agreed. "I surrender. Okay. Dinner."

"Great. I know a great place by the sea out at Byblos. Won't be crowded or touristy this time of year. Come to think of it, it's probably closed too. Oh well, how does Italian sound? Night view of Pigeon Rocks?"

"Whatever," Chloe giggled. "I'll leave it up to you. Six o'clock, in the lobby?"

"Done," Kevin agreed. "Gotta run now, though. See you tonight."

(49)

A current of sultry air flickered the candle flame as Chloe and Kevin huddled over their small table. The sea was not far away. Shadows momentarily danced across their faces.

"Hmm. This is wonderful, Chris," Chloe purred, sipping a Bekah Valley burgundy. "The food, the wine, the night."

"I thought you might like it, Jenny," Kevin grinned.

The moon set low and orange into the Mediterranean darkness beyond the Pigeon Rock formations that mark the western end of the city. A miniature fishing boat fleet cast bands of bright light writhing on the shadowed waves.

"The light attracts fish at night," Kevin pointed out.

Chloe mused softly, "It reminds me of when I was a little girl. Life seemed endless then."

"It's endless now," Kevin whispered. Chloe smiled.

A sound of distant gunfire rattled briefly like an ancient cough. They huddled closer, reminded of the fleeting preciousness of life.

(50)

The long white lace curtains stirred in the breeze that gently disarranged Chloe's hair as she slept in Kevin's hotel bed. Sun rays splintered the walls with ivory slivers. Kevin tucked his shirt in, slipped on his shoes and stooped to give the girl a kiss on the cheek.

"Mmm?" she stirred.

"I have a few merchants and businessmen to meet this morning," Kevin lied. "I'll meet you for lunch downstairs in the lobby at ... one?"

"Mmm," Chloe agreed snuggling deeper into the luxurious covers.

Kevin closed the door gently. He whistled softly as he walked to the elevator.

Outside the entrance doors a clutter of taxis waited. Kevin slipped into one and gave the driver an address, Akwar. A half hour later the taxi pulled up near the wall of the American Embassy. Kevin got out and walked inconspicuously to a side entrance. A marine nodded at his credentials and allowed him passage. At reception, he asked to see a certain gentleman and after a short wait was passed through an inner checkpoint. He conferred with his contact in a comfortable lime green air-conditioned office with little view beyond the iron grills on the windows.

A short while later, the suited man thanked Kevin for his report and left, allowing Kevin to wait undisturbed as the morning hours whiled away. As the clock hands approached noon, Kevin got up and left as he had come, unnoticed. Taxis were frequent in the area and after a short walk, he flagged one down and returned to the Hilton.

(51)

A waiter brought a second whiskey and soda. Kevin sat impatiently watching Lebanese television mutedly flashing Al Jazeera news clips – the Ukraine war was dominant, interspersed with sporadic colorful commercials. Beer, swim suits, soft drinks. At one forty-five he strode to the lobby desk.

"Are there any messages for Christopher Josephs?" he asked. "Room 85".

The attractive dark-haired woman reached into the appropriate pigeon hole key box and handed Kevin a folded piece of hotel stationary.

"Mr. Josephs."

"Thank you," Kevin replied. He opened the note. It was from Chloe, as expected.

"Chris darling," the delicate script began. "I was called unexpectedly to return to Zurich. Thanks for last night." It was signed, "XOX Jen."

Kevin beckoned the woman.

"Sir?"

"See if you can book me on a flight to London tonight," he asked politely. "I'll be in my room." He returned to his room and began packing his few belongings. Immediately, the phone rang. It was the front desk.

"Mr. Josephs, there is an MEA flight that makes connection with Easy Jet after a one hour lay-over in Athens. It is leaving seven p.m. and arriving at London-Gatwick early in the morning. There are plenty of seats available. Shall I book you on this one?"

"That will be fine," Kevin replied. "Shoukran."

"Afwan, Mr. Josephs."

(52)

"Yes, Lindsey," Kevin answered wearily. "I can hear you fine."

"We have decided to keep you onto the Sparrow affair. Give her a few weeks, then run into her again. But probably not in Beirut this time. Zurich, whatever. Make your own choice but be convincing and keep your relationship," he searched for the appropriate word, "flowering. Do you understand?"

"Yes Mr. Merric, I think I understand," Kevin replied evenly. "You want me to make contact again. Did I get it on the first try?"

"Yes, Kevin, you got it right," Lindsey answered. His grimace somehow echoed across the wires.

"Well, great. I must be improving. Keep it in mind when performance reviews come up, please. Nice talking with you again."

Kevin hurried to hang up, but Lindsey caught him with a shout. "Just a minute, Kevin!"

Kevin stared blankly at the receiver. "Fifty-eight seconds," he answered.

"Very funny. Everyone wants to be a comedian. Ha, ha. Now listen. This relationship with the girl, let it blossom. Go along with her feelings, ideas, political convictions, etcetera, etcetera. Show dissatisfaction with your own life, your work, employers, pay, etcetera, etcetera. Make yourself valuable to her. Do you understand?"

"I understand, etcetera, etcetera," Kevin retorted.

"Good boy," Lindsey smirked twisting an imaginary needle. Kevin hated being called boy. "I'm giving you six months. See if you can penetrate the

Xenox Organization in that time." The phone clicked off leaving the line buzzing.

"Right," Kevin fumed "Oh and goodbye to you too, son of a bitch." He stepped from the secure embassy telephone booth and studied the sight out the hallway window. Fog, mizzling rain, traffic. London, what else is new? He sighed and walked on his way.

(53)

Kevin leaned hard against the rudder handle as the miniscule sailing skiff stalled against a stiff burst of oncoming wind. White caps flecked the lake waters under an impossibly blue sky. The blinding sun flashed through the flapping jib sail. The mainsail boom lurched. Kevin ducked as the hard wood spar narrowly missed his head. Clunk.

Oh, my goodness. He had clumsily run into his neighbor's dinghy. These lakes are always so crowded. In December? Kevin hurried to the bow, big red eyes, tongue out, tail wagging. How better to make an awkward apology?

Well, heaven help us all. Chloe, I mean, Jennifer. I didn't know you liked to sail too. And of all the frozen lakes in all the world you just happened to float in on mine. And we just happened to be boating on the same one at the same time of day. Gosh, what a coincidence.

Kevin lounged in his Bayswater apartment not far from his embassy. He struggled to his feet and shuffled over to a small drinks refrigerator. He selected Perrier soda water, poured half and half with orange juice, and returned to his armchair. He flicked the remote and the television hummed to life with a quiver of static.

A volcano was bubbling in some long-forgotten land where dinosaur birds flapped in the smoky sky, ITV. He flipped through the channels briefly halting on Al Jazeera English and Moscow RTV to get a few clips of news. Putin, Biden, Ukraine. The slowly fading focus of the Queen's passing. She would be eternally missed and mourned by most of the world, but life moves on. The House of Commons was on BBC II in a typical pandemonium of yeas and nays. On BBC I, Sir So and So was reminiscing on the British Monarchy and fretting over the role it should play in today's troubled world of unemployment and infrastructure overload. Would Charles ever be able to replace the unifying and solid presence his mother portrayed? He poked the off button. The tube died with a sigh and a vanishing bright dot.

"For this girl, "just happened" won't do," he mumbled to himself.

[54]

The descending escalator carried Chloe along with the crowd towards the ticket booths and the turnstiles to the trains. Kevin pushed his way through the bustling railway station not far behind. He followed her as she boarded a train from the airport to downtown Zurich. As the train creaked forward, he approached the girl sitting alone, anonymously huddled behind her tinted glasses. He took the adjoining seat.

"Ah, there you are again," he declared confidently.

She started, recognized and exclaimed, "Oh my God. Chris Josephs." She eyed him suspiciously. "What are you doing here? Are you following me?"

"As a matter of fact," Kevin replied, "no." He paused innocently, then added, "Not really, that is. But I did come here just to see you again."

"How did you know I was arriving today?" she asked with a doubtful look.

"Well, actually," Kevin explained. "That wasn't so easy. I called the airlines, but with this damned security, I couldn't get an answer. 'I'm sorry, sir, we cannot give out that information', is all they would say. I know I met you on that Beirut Lufthansa flight, that you travel twice a month with connections on Swiss International and live in Zurich. I just did my calculations, some educated guess work and hung out at arrivals. I kind of pegged you for a schedule, and here you are." He paused, "Two days late, but here none-the-less."

"You've got to be kidding. You waited around the airport for two days?" she asked incredulously.

"I guess you could put it like that," Kevin answered.

"I see," Chloe pondered this darkly.

"By the way, Jennifer Newton," Kevin smiled, "You were registered at the Hilton as Chloe Tanyas. So, which is which?"

"Chloe," Chloe admitted.

Kevin leaned over and kissed her lightly on the lips. "Pleased to meet you, Chloe."

"Oh Chris, what are you doing here?" she pouted.

"It's very simple. I can't get you out of my mind."

"Oh, for heaven's sake," Chloe moaned.

"No, really," Kevin said seriously. "Can't sleep, we had something there that night in Beirut."

Chloe relaxed and glanced out the window as the rush hour traffic ran hesitatingly along the autobahn, bumper to bumper. "Yes," she agreed sadly, "Yes, we did."

The train jerked as the brakes clenched the wheels briefly, then released. The cars jolted to a standstill as an express train thundered by on an adjacent track. Kevin sighed inwardly with relief. Phase one, the most delicate, was complete.

[55]

Kevin leaned hard against the rudder handle as the miniscule sailing skiff stalled against a stiff burst of oncoming wind. White puffs streaked the lake surface under an impossibly blue sky. The blinding sun flashed through the flapping jib sail. The mainsail boom lurched. Kevin ducked as the hard wood spar narrowly missed his head. Clunk.

The ice skiff toppled over spilling Kevin and Chloe onto the ice. They spun helplessly along the frozen lake. Chloe laughed uncontrollably.

"I thought you said you knew how to do this," she sputtered with tears in her eyes.

"I did. I do," Kevin asserted, standing precariously and dusting off the snow.

(56)

"Ice sailing," Kevin said. "It's like water sailing but the boat has skates, Mr. Merric. Water, you know, that bluish stuff that you always see so much of in the oceans." Garbled noises responded from the telephone. "Yes, well we all have our opinions, you know. Well, you want it to look authentic. Okay, this is as authentic as you can get. All I need is for you to cover the expenses, thank you." He hung up quickly.

"What a miserable way to make a living," he muttered. But what was really troubling him was he knew this was not just about making a living. Not this time, and that worried him deeply.

(57)

The sun radiated a gentle warmth into the glassed veranda where Kevin sat overlooking the Limmat River as it glided icily and serenely through Zurich. The café table was discreetly bordered with potted plants. The afternoon light of early spring was liquid and still.

"I'm tired of this life," he said to Chloe who sat opposite him.

"We all are from time to time," she agreed sympathetically. "But things could be worse," she added cheerfully looking around with a smile.

"No, not this life, I mean me, my life. The work I'm doing, serving the almighty order, following along in lockstep day to day, doing whatever I'm told to do, all that. I mean we're all pawns, but I can't help looking at the damage the gold and copper industry, for instance, has done around the world, cyanide leeching processing, for example. Have you ever seen or even heard of what "acidic mine drainage" does to a village water supply? It's a nice antiseptic industry term for toxic water contaminated with residual heavy metals. Things the mining company glosses over up until the moment they cut and run."

"Then, when they're gone and the seepage starts in earnest, it's someone else's problem. The corrupt governments make so much money off the deals that no one goes after the polluters. You see it everywhere, not just third world countries. In the American western states, people are so trusting of their own superiority, they don't even see what's being finagled under their own noses in broad daylight. That's all for South American banana republics, not the good old USA. Same for Europe, until there's a spill in a river or something."

"So here I am sacrificing my individuality and self-respect to feed the great beast its daily bread of precious metals." Kevin shrugged.

"Corny," Chloe stated before she could stop herself. "No, I mean," she began.

"No, no. You're right. It is. The perfect world is always somewhere, out of reach." He sighed. "But I really am a bit weary with it all."

"You could always Occupy something, or put on a yellow jacket and stand by the road with a sign," she said with a laugh, then touched his arm and excused herself. "I'll be back in a minute."

Kevin watched her sway between empty tables and disappear into the inner shadows of the café. He stretched with a lazy yawn. Yes, he was tired of it, more so than Chloe could ever imagine, more than he could honestly admit even to himself, more than was innocently permissible. Ever since he began the charade with this beautiful girl, he had recklessly allowed his thoughts to roam.

Maybe it was possible. Maybe he could get out of it all, and go away somewhere. God knew, he didn't give a hoot about Lindsey Merric and the entire organizational structure the man represented. He had once, when they had recruited him out of his graduate studies in international politics, but that was a long time ago. Experience had mellowed his youthful feelings some years back. Now it was just a job he knew and performed well, and he enjoyed the perks, of course. Those would be hard to replace.

Kevin loved the freedom his job offered. The opportunity to exist beyond and above the law was exhilarating. He represented the law's final desperation, its belief in its own righteousness above all else. He was one of the tools the law used for overstepping its own sanctified rules in the name of that righteousness. And that made him free. He always wondered how he would feel if and when it all came to an end.

Kevin hated counting the deaths he had been responsible for in the line of duty; "in the line of duty", what a phrase, great for soothing the conscience. But he kept a tally anyway, he couldn't help himself. Twenty, something? He couldn't be sure anymore, the hell with it.

An attractive waitress startled Kevin. "Coffee?" He smiled and nodded. The girl poured fresh brew into his cup and waddled away promiscuously flaunting her buttocks. Kevin grinned and slipped back into his reverie.

Free? Yes, to an extent. He had the world at his fingertips to roam in, on assignment, of course. And assignments had taken him from Afghanistan to Hong Kong, from Moscow to Johannesburg, from Beijing to Sydney. He was close to fluent in French, passable in

German and Spanish, and could at least communicate in several other languages and dialects. He could pop in and out of cultures with the ease that many people did visiting neighboring towns. But since the advent of the Internet, this was no longer as unique a trait as it once had been. Kids could do all that nowadays, with more ease and more current knowledge.

What did he have to show for all the heady days? Friends? Not a one. Only an ever-dwindling pool of acquaintances and colleagues seemed to linger on. Every time he turned around, another girl got married, someone died, someone was killed. Fortune? Not much, enough to cover the living expenses of the eternal present, with a bit extra, of course, set aside unofficially and against regulations. He had accumulated a sizable amount of "retirement funds" by everyday standards, stashed safely away in a Swiss account, but it wasn't quite as significant or as satisfyingly great as he had expected after the long years of service work. One consolation was that he had distanced himself from relatives. He had none left living that he knew of. In that way, he was free.

Chloe emerged back into the sunlit gallery. She stopped to speak with the head waiter, someone she knew. Kevin watched her closely. Maybe with this one it could be possible.

He couldn't be an asset of value forever. Times change and young fighters, fresh, ambitious and locked in sync with the future, step in. An unexpected power shuffle or a simple twist of game rules could push this old timer aside in a flicker of an eye. Eventually, the pale of obsolescence would triumph. It always did. He had long decided to be prepared for the inevitable.

Chloe approached the table with a smile. Kevin felt his official assignment, this dutiful romantic fantasy, slipping from charade into a reality he had unconsciously sought for many years.

"Let's go, Chris. Before the clouds block out all of our sunshine."

Kevin glanced over his shoulder at the light, a brief respite in the cloudy days of winter. He looked back at Chloe with her corona of golden hair, the sun in his cloudy life. He stood.

(58)

"I love Van Gogh," Chloe announced standing back from the glimmer of the "Sunflowers".

Kevin shrugged. "He was rejected and a bit despised by most everyone in his own lifetime. He sold, what? Only one painting while he was alive. Was subject to depressions and rages, and finally committed suicide."

"Sad," Chloe sighed. "You would think that someone would've understood."

"Would you have?" Kevin asked wryly.

Chloe gave him a light kiss on the cheek. "No, Chris darling. I probably wouldn't have."

Kevin groaned. "Charming. Oh, the price one pays for fame and a pedestal in history."

"But I still like his paintings," she added thoughtfully.

They pressed their way through the security turnstiles, shuffled through the incoming troops of tourists, and exited the British National Museum onto a damp Trafalgar Square.

"Still here, after all these years," Kevin said hailing one of London's famous black taxicabs. A maroon coloured one pulled to the curb.

"The lions, or the taxis?" Chloe asked hustling into her seat.

"The foggy dew," Kevin answered. He kissed her. "Glad we could meet at my place this time."

- - -

"Ice sailing, Lake Zurich. Skiing, San Moritz, Zermatt. Sightseeing, London, Copenhagen, Amsterdam. Eurostar to Paris. Car rental, Venice to Cannes. Overnight train back to Zurich, and again Paris." Lindsey tapped the papers.

"He's having himself a time of it alright," Gloria commented.

"I'll say," Lindsey grunted.

"Must be nice."

"Nice. Yes, I'm sure. Bloody expensive, too," Lindsey continued. "But at least there seems to be some evidence of progress."

"I wondered how much?" Gloria ventured, snidely. The jest was lost on Lindsey.

"Difficult to say at this stage," Lindsey said pensively. He reluctantly added, "All we can do is give him free reign and lots of rope and hope he doesn't hang himself with it, along with the mission."

(59)

The traffic crawled along the Boulevard Saint Germaine where Chloe and Kevin nuzzled in a cab. "I'm going to be late," Chloe moaned eyeing the drizzling afternoon.

"Plenty of time," Kevin reassured her. "Rush hour will thin out in half an hour."

"Fine for you. My plane leaves in just over an hour. Not boards, leaves," Chloe complained anxiously gesturing at her delicate wristwatch. It was Beirut again. "Are you sure you can't come along?" she asked for the tenth time.

"No," Kevin insisted. "I would never be able to explain it." He thought of Lindsey's face if he did go. "I really need to be in London this week. I'll meet you when you return to Zurich."

"I mentioned you to Mr. Xenox," Chloe said offhandedly.

"Uh huh," Kevin responded with fake distraction. His interest peaked sharply but he kept it well concealed. "And?"

"And he wants to meet you."

Kevin followed a raindrop trickling at an angle down the taxicab window devouring other drops and growing in size and speed as it went. It fluttered away in a blast of wind as the vehicle picked up speed. Traffic was thinning out. "The space between us, fill it up," Kevin thought. And the job was back.

"What do you think?" he asked her.

"Oh, Christopher. You know what I think. It would be wonderful. We would work as a team. We could go everywhere together," Chloe answered excitedly.

"Yes," Kevin agreed.

The cabbie blared on his horn and cursed at his window. "Merde! Imbecile!" He grinned a sheepish apology at his passengers.

"Okay. How soon then?" Kevin asked.

"When I get back from Lebanon. I'll only be a night in Zurich, then I leave straight for Manhattan. A week, maybe two at the most. I'll keep you posted. You can meet me there." Chloe smiled.

"Okay," Kevin agreed. "Sounds great. Call my cell. I'll probably be at my flat. Just let me know when."

(60)

Kevin cheerfully pushed open the blue metal door that lead into a small laboratory in an anonymous Canary Wharf basement. He wore a trim grey suit and carried a slim briefcase, a cameo of a legitimate businessman visiting London. An attractive girl looked up from her desk.

"Hi, Marie. Long time no see," he beamed.

"Oh, 'allo Mr. Kevin," the young technician answered with a heavy Chelsea accent. "'ere now, where've you been lately?"

"Here and there, as usual, and how many times do I have to keep telling you, stop calling me Mister," Kevin retorted pinching her on the cheek. "So good to see you, Luv. Want a cuppa?"

"Now you stop that Mr. Kevin!" the girl howled, laughing.

Kevin peered around the dimly lit room. Various oddities, weapons, chemical bottles, test tubes, pipettes and the like were scattered on shelves and tables, tools of the information gathering and scientific analysis trade.

He opened his brief case on a table and extracted a sheaf of reports which he handed to the girl.

"Here's some mementos or at least memos from the office. Timothy's on vacation again?" he asked.

"Always is," she replied. "Or so it seems."

Kevin spied a familiar pale red hued plastic block near a sink. He reached across a jumble of instruments to retrieve it. "Ah," he exclaimed. "The Libyan gelignite. That is what it is, isn't it?"

Marie swung around in her swivel chair. "That? Hmm, yes, that's what it is, very 'igh explosives." She fished out a form from a drawer file. "Let's see, 'ere we go, a special amalgamation of TNT and RDX, Pentaerythritol Tetranitrate, sometimes referred to as Pentolite, or Hexogen, or Cyclonite. Take your pick. I guess it all depends on who's making it. It happens to be ultra-powerful in this specific mixture, but inert as a biscuit as it is. Perfectly 'armless and a bit hard to detect from the outside, sealed like so in that paraffin plastic. It needs a detonator to do any damage. Maybe that's what the circular indentation on the one side is for. Funny, you don't see it in that form generally. Usually, we'd expect it in larger bundles."

"That's what I thought when I took it," Kevin replied tossing it from one hand to the other. "Mind if I take it along for a spell to mull over?"

"You go right a'ead. We already did our report on it. Better bring it back eventually, though. I'll make a note 'ere that you've got it. Anyway, it's just one more piece of junk clutterin' up the place," she said pivoting back to her work.

Kevin placed the block in his case and snapped it shut. He snuck up and grabbed the girl from behind. She squealed.

"Still getting married?" he asked, "or can I change your mind?"

"Not anymore, dear." Marie flashed a gold and diamond speckled ring.

"Oh no," Kevin moaned. "What a tragedy." He formally kissed her hand. "My deepest condolences," he said mournfully. "Didn't anyone warn the groom?" He dodged a metal ruler as he exited into the basement hallway.

[61]

Dean checked off another semi-truckload of completed and packaged vibration meters; destination: StresChek, Chicago. "Chicago is getting its fair share," he said to himself, strolling over to the foreman's office. Sam was busy behind a mound of buzz work papers.

"Okay, Sam," Dean announced coming through the doorway. "That's the last of the Chicago lot for today."

Sam nodded without looking up. Dean poured himself half a paper cup of coffee dregs. "Damn", he thought and flipped the lot into the trash. He fumbled with the coffee maker and emptied the used filter complete with wet grains neatly onto the dustbin's edge. It slid to the floor. "Damn," he grumbled, slipping the litter under the counter with his shoe while trying to separate a single filter from a tightly packed fresh stack. He partially succeeded and poured most of a new packet of coffee into an unintentionally doubled filter. The rest joined the mess on the floor. He filled the water heating compartment and raced to force the Pyrex pot into its slot, but the steaming water was quicker and poured sizzling coffee onto the hot plate. "Damn."

Sam looked up. "You okay?"

"Fine," Dean grumbled.

"I count fifteen trucks to Chicago this week. How does that match with your figures?"

Dean glanced at his clipboard. "Fifteen, on the nose," he answered. He poured himself a cup of grainy beverage. "Damn, who makes these contraptions?" He checked his notes again. Chicago, New York, Houston, Atlanta, San Francisco, etc, etc. "Lots of shipments," he marveled silently to himself. "Lots of meters. That's quite a profit." He exited the office through the doorway into the assembly warehouse. Ahmed saw him and signaled. Dean walked over to his bench.

"How's it going, kid?"

"Great," Ahmed said testily.

"Look," Dean explained patiently. "All we can do is wait and see what happens next. Just do your job for now. Okay? Make a little money and relax."

Ahmed groaned. "I know you are right, but for how long?"

"As long as necessary, kid," Dean replied.

(62)

Kevin tapped out his pass code and slipped into the landing of his apartment building. He rapped his mailbox. It responded hollowly empty as usual. A door cracked open behind him.

"Yes, Mrs. Wickersham, lovely day, lovely weather," Kevin said without turning around. He bounded up the stairs and ducked towards his doorway on the next landing. "Nosey old gal," he murmured passing into his rooms.

He whistled a popular tune that had been lingering from a radio program earlier in the day, tossed his coat on a dining table chair, undid his tie, kicked his shoes off into a corner, and flicked the television set on with the remote, all in a continuous ballet of relaxation. He pulled the curtains aside to expose a fragile English sunset, poured himself a full vodka tonic lime drink, and flipped open his briefcase on the coffee table.

He noticed the pale red plastic tablet of explosives on top of his papers and picked it up. He weighed it absently in his hands, glancing around for somewhere to put it. His eyes lighted on a space on a mostly crowded bookshelf. He slipped it snugly between two paperbacks.

With a sigh, he flopped into a comfortable chair to flip through the news channels.

- - -

The news ended. The last channel Kevin had been watching descended into a blur of an outdated talk show, a quick comedy, commercials, and some ambiguous commentaries. The news reappeared briefly, followed by a prehistoric black and white war film of no discernible character. The screen went fuzzy after a rendition of God Save the Queen or America the Beautiful depending on who was listening; this station still signed off in the wee hours of the night. Kevin slept in his recliner suffused in a grey static glow and lulled by the soft hiss emanating from the television.

Rain drops spattered against the windowpanes as a thick layer of clouds settled over the darkened city. A window, left slightly ajar to allow a fresh flow of air into the apartment, quivered in the draft. Kevin stirred in his armchair. The sound of a late-night vehicle sizzled by on the wet tarmac below. The window shook more loudly with a stronger gust and rattled its hinges. Its weather damped curtain snapped sharply.

Kevin woke. Ruffled and disoriented, he glanced nervously and rapidly around the room. But as he regained awareness and conscious familiarity, he rose, relaxed and yawned heartily. "Home," he sighed contentedly. He latched the window and gazed around the comfortable flat ticking off familiar objects in his mind. Each had its own special memory; the Persian rug, a brass Arabian coffee pot, a sheathed Gurkha knife, a Samurai sword, a strange Thai stringed instrument, a small Picasso etching splashed with colour. The interior vibrated with shadows cast by the flickering television screen. He looked at the bookshelves, reconsidering a possible rearrangement he had been contemplating since he had moved in some years ago. It would never happen he knew but it was fun to think about. He scanned along the book line and stopped at the pinkish red block of explosives from the Libyan Desert.

He stared vaguely at the block nestled cozily in amongst the books. Memories taunted him and eventually teased out a dismembered image, nearly forgotten amongst so many others. A turquoise blue box sat atop the shiny glass surface of an official looking desk. It was some kind of a plastic hood with a recording meter. There was a cylinder, wires and terminals, weren't there? And an empty slot.

"What is this vacant area here?" someone asked.

"The battery package goes in there," a voice answered. A hand with thick stubby fingers reached across Kevin's memory and glided a couple of paperback books neatly into the unfilled space. "Like this."

The Night

(63)

Sheldon fumbled with his lighter nervously, briefly flicking sparks and a wavering flame. Quitting smoking was more difficult than he ever anticipated. He snapped the lighter shut and inhaled deeply as if dragging in a lungful of precious nicotine. He exhaled slowly. "My God," he stammered. "What are we going to do?"

Gloria shuffled her neat stack of papers as if magically resolving the changed situation. "We have miscalculated the true circumstances," she said hesitantly.

"No kidding," Sheldon exclaimed. "No frigging kidding! It's been well over six months since this operation went into full swing. The entire diplomatic world is focused on the situation in Ukraine, and now this. They'll have nearly every major bridge, freeway overpass, tunnel or whatever in every city in the country mined by now. We can't go in to remove these damn devices. Any move on our part will just tip them off that we're on to them. If the controllers of this scheme even suspect we know…"

"There will be nothing preventing them from blowing the entire lot." Scott filled in as Sheldon's voice tapered off. "Can they do that? Can they?"

Lindsey Merric nodded, "Oh yeah, Sheldon. They can do that. They certainly can do that." Silence descended on the small group as their thoughts struggled in the void.

"So obvious, so obvious," Sheldon mumbled involuntarily.

"Yes," Lindsey interjected, "too obvious to see. While everyone in Homeland Security and the National Security Agency, not to mention Interpol and most of the rest of the world's security systems, have their noses buried up their asses in their computers and their damn heads floating in the Internet Cloud looking for Cyber-attacks and what not, this happens, in real time no less. What the hell! Isn't anyone living in real time anymore?"

The others turned, waiting for his direction. The case chief bravely faced his subordinates with determination. "Damn, how could this happen? Our options…"

"Total disruption of land traffic in America," Sheldon blurted out. Panic was replacing shock as the reality of the threat persisted. "This'll do it. This'll really do it. This'll take all stops out everywhere internationally. It's total meltdown for sure. Who cares if the electrical grid gets tampered with when the entire infrastructure is in shambles? If America collapses from within, what can we expect from Russia? A perfect scenario for an attack on NATO? Where would the world power balance go from there? This'll just be icing on the cake for these people."

Lindsey slammed both palms on the table startling the group into silence. Gloria winced and stopped in mid shuffle. "For the love of God," he growled angrily. "Get ahold of yourselves."

Scott stared blankly at him. "You know what this means as well as we do. The tornadoes, the hurricanes, the offshore oil fire disasters, earthquakes, tsunamis, climate change wildfires and floods - they won't even compare to this. Nothing will. Look at the anger and mayhem we get just from oil spills, not to mention oil and natural gas shortages. What happens when there's plenty of oil but hundreds of thousands of miles of dead-end roads? Busted gas pipelines, electricity and communication towers down, railway bridges collapsed? The place will go crazy!" His eyes took on a deep feverish glow.

Sheldon had been holding back but his imagination began to squeeze involuntary words from his mouth. "No moving traffic. People stranded on the streets. Airports at a standstill. Crowds, no, hordes of looters. And what's the percentage of Americans nowadays carrying guns? How many private caches of automatic assault weapons are scattered about? The cities will be battlegrounds. The police will be outnumbered. You think those 'I can't breathe' riots were something? Not even a full military intervention will be able to take control of this one."

"And who would be there to control the armed forces even if they could?" Scott added ominously.

"Now listen!" Lindsey grumbled loudly. "No one outside this room and," he added bitterly, "Kevin in London knows anything about this." He slowly repeated, "No one," and paused. "Our first objective is to keep it that way. Is that clear?"

He gazed hard at Gloria who returned his look and nodded. Sheldon stared back blankly but grunted an affirmation. Scott uttered a gruff "Yeah, yeah, clear as can be."

"Alright. Now, this Xenox has to be the lynchpin. He is central to all our investigations and Sparrow's movements so far. First question; what could be his motives? He's making hundreds of millions of dollars just on the Traffic Safety Bill and the legal sale of these StresChek products. Why risk all that? What the devil is he up to?"

"So, this isn't about money," Gloria nervously offered.

"Right," Lindsey agreed. "How could it be? He's already got enough to buy the world a few times over."

"Revenge?" Scott blurted.

"Revenge," Lindsey repeated pensively. "Yes, possibly. My thoughts exactly."

"Ransom?" Sheldon ventured, but quickly corrected himself. "But that gets back to money."

"Not necessarily," Lindsey reminded him. "There's also political ransom, the releasing of prisoners, toppling governments and such. It's one of the main motives for terror activities today."

"Blackmail?" Gloria guessed. "Maybe he's got some demands?"

"But who for?" Scott asked. "Xenox isn't Palestinian. He's Greek. At least he was."

Lindsey shook his head wearily. "Palestinians aren't the only ones with friends behind bars. Nor are they the only people trying to focus media attention onto their cause. There's Chechnya, Islamic State, the Syrian and African refugees, hundreds of others."

"Maybe he wants to draw attention to something else then," Sheldon stammered.

"Maybe, Shel," Lindsey mused. "Maybe. But what?" He ran his fingers through his hair and wiped a bead of sweat from his forehead. "Is there anything else anyone can think of that might be going on here?" he asked.

The small group was sullen and silent, barely looking at each other.

"No," he continued. "I don't think so either. I can't see anything but revenge, ransom or blackmail, and maybe publicity."

"Which is more likely?" Sheldon asked.

"That," Lindsey answered, "is what we must find out. Revenge? Why? Against America? The West? The world? What could have happened in Xenox's life to seed such anger?"

Gloria whispered inaudibly to Sheldon.

"There's something you wish to share with all of us, Gloria?" Lindsey demanded.

"I ... uh ... I just said ..."

"She said he wants to control the world," Sheldon mumbled. "Power, we forgot power."

Lindsey rubbed his forehead. This was beginning to hurt. "Yes," he mused. "We certainly did. We forgot power."

"The Illuminati," Scott whispered.

"The what?" Lindsey asked incredulously. "The ... the Illuminati? Are you totally nuts? Is that the best you can do? You can't be serious!"

Gloria muffled a gasp.

"Of course, why not?" Sheldon asked. "Conspiracy theory has been pointing in that direction for years. The breakdown of societies worldwide, it's already occurring. The disintegration of the Levant; Israel alienating itself from all other countries of the world; the collapse of the Western empires; the refugee invasions; total destruction of environment; corporate genetic control of the food supply; monetary failure; globalization; all the ingredients are there. This could be the final push to get the ball rolling. Over the edge we go! World domination would just be part of the mop up operations!"

"Okay, okay, okay!" Lindsey said forcibly. "Enough of this nonsense. No one knows if this Illuminati even exists. What bunk! It's all fairy tales to keep the populace confused as far as anyone can tell. Let's keep this in the realm of reality, can we?"

Scott mumbled something that only he was privy to.

"Yes? Scott. Please share," Lindsey said quietly.

"Just Zionism," Scott replied, "and the Yinon Plan for the disruption and breakdown of the Western democracies. It's all there, if you look at it."

"Just Zionism," Lindsey repeated. "The Yinon Plan. A Greek-American Zionist madman?"

The table erupted momentarily with everyone trying to say something at once, then fell silent just as fast.

"Thank you. Thank you very much," Lindsey said as quiet settled again. "That's very helpful, Zionism and the Illuminati ... very helpful." He paused. "Damn, this is just what we need at our backs with all attention focused on Russia and Ukraine, the Islamic State and the disintegrations in Syria and Iraq, the Iranian nuclear ambitions and Israel primping for war with them, and meanwhile China jabbing at its neighbor's borders while Afghanistan returns to the stone age, new virus outbreaks, hunger. Wonderful. Damn! Double damn! We're getting hit from all sides, and now from the inside. Illuminati, indeed!"

The quiet began to ring painfully. "We need to find direction," Lindsey finally said.

(64)

"Direction?" Kevin stopped in his tracks and looked about himself. He was at a crossing in Victoria Embankment Gardens by Waterloo Bridge.

"To the Tower," an attractive tourist girl from the continent was asking. "Do you know the direction?"

He stared blankly at her. He had been wandering the streets for hours passing through all the familiar haunts of central London. He was avoiding going to the Embassy. He wasn't sure if he could keep a pleasant façade of cheerful banter going with his cohorts under these new circumstances.

"Direction?" he repeated. "I have no direction. There is no direction."

The girl flipped her hair and strutted off in a huff. Kevin crossed over to Cleopatra's Needle and gazed at the ancient Egyptian obelisk and the Thames beyond. He leaned against a railing and watched the famous dirty old river rolling by. It was already evening and a splendid Waterloo sunset was beginning as the day's clouds dissipated. Kevin shook his head. He didn't feel much like he was in paradise at the moment. He caught a vague glimpse of something blue attached under the supports of Waterloo Bridge, but paid it no mind. It was a bit distant.

(65)

"Kevin Varyte," Gloria was the next to break the silence.

"Yes," Lindsey repeated, "Kevin Varyte. We have Kevin." He paused momentarily. "Alright now, to summarize we have our peripheral players, a macabre scenario, and central to everything is Xenox."

"And the plot?" Scott responded.

"Blackmail, revenge, ransom, publicity and/or power," Sheldon replied.

"Yes, but which one?" Gloria asked meekly.

"That is our problem – which one. We're going to have to dig into our Mr. Xenox's history, present and past, in a lot more detail," Lindsey soberly continued. "For starters who does he know who might be locked up in prison somewhere, Brasil, Greece, here in the US, or anywhere in the world? What causes could he be supporting?" He looked at Scott, "Palestinians? Maybe so."

Scott cleared his throat.

"Regardless," Lindsey carried on. "We have an unlimited data base at our disposal. I assume the Agency has been able to keep it current. I want any and all cross-references checked and reported. Anything that links to Xenox no matter how ambiguously has got to be scrutinized, business contacts, finance, travel, whatever. Electronic surveillance has turned up nothing we have noticed, no suspicious e-correspondence, illegal business activity, yes, but terroristic intentions - zip. This is immediate priority, but we can't tip our hand. It's urgent but it has to be kept under wraps."

"That's going to be … difficult," Sheldon stammered.

Scott began to say something but Lindsey cut him short. "We have to stall this at any cost. A breach would be disastrous. Each of us has plenty of staff manpower who can operate on a need-to-know basis. Put a good cover-story on it. Xenox is an easy target, suspected transgressions over national security, smuggling offenses, financial fraud. Smother any subordinate curiosity and stonewall all questions. We have leeway here, and authority. Use it. We can't afford any leaks."

The others voiced agreement. "And Kevin?" Gloria prodded.

(66)

Kevin sat in the cafeteria with a croissant and a cup of black coffee. He had finally worked up the courage to return to the embassy with enough confidence not to reveal his panicked thoughts. It was a challenge. The end-game scenarios would not stop playing out in his mind. "This just isn't going away," he said abstractedly.

"You don't say," said Jim taking a seat across from Kevin. "What's not going away?" The canteen room was nearly empty. It was past evening, and just a couple of night shift owls were hunched over discussions and snacks at a corner spot.

Kevin gave a short start. "Oh, hi. Uh, the weather," he said gaining composure. "Looks like rain for a while, eh?"

"That it does old Kev. That it does. What else? It's England, you know. You're here a bit late tonight."

Kevin nodded, "I've got some catch up work."

"That would explain the black coffee. That'll keep you up all night."

Kevin nodded again. "I don't need the coffee for that," he thought to himself. "End of the month stuff," he replied.

"Tell me about it," the junior officer said.

"Sometime later perhaps. Well, I better get at it," Kevin said excusing himself. He headed towards his cubicle for some privacy. "All I can do now is wait to hear from Langley," he concluded.

(67)

"Yes," Lindsey drawled. "Kevin." He paused in the expectant silence. Now was the time to update the others on that end of the matter. "Kevin has been meeting with Chloe, our Sparrow, regularly for approximately six months now, basically since just after our last meeting. I thought it might be wise to cultivate a physical connection. It looks like it was the right thing to do."

The others glanced at each other. "You mean," Sheldon began.

"Yes," Lindsey cut him short. "I mean I instructed him to strike up a relationship with her. His first contact with her was in Beirut when she returned to her familiar travel schedule after her Libyan detour."

"So," Scott said musing it over. "Six months. That's quite a while."

"Agreed. Now I hope it will pay off. We have certainly invested in this effort. I indicated we needed to get close to the Xenox operations and that meant an ongoing relationship, a tryst if you will."

"A romantic affair?" Sheldon asked. "We weren't told."

"Correct. This was a low-key assignment. We all know the rules here. But knowing our Kevin and what we've seen of Miss Tanya's photographs and record, I imagine that was not a difficult challenge for him."

"Or unpleasant," added Scott wryly.

Lindsey grunted and motioned to Gloria who handed him a file from her precious hoard of papers. "Six months," he repeated reading the file. "Zurich, London, Paris, Venice. Skiing, Zermatt. Glacier hiking and ice climbing, Mt. Blanc. Copenhagen, Berlin. Etcetera, etcetera." He looked up. "I won't bore you with the details. In short, over this time period up to the present, Kevin has expressed dissatisfaction with his cover-story employment as a representative for industrial precious metals and mining concerns, buying and selling. An excellent cover, if I may say, arranged by myself."

Scott glanced briefly at Sheldon.

Lindsey continued, "Let's see now. Expressed disgust with Euro-American political establishments. Showed pro-Palestinian sentiments, frustration with the West's response to the Arab Spring uprisings and resultant government blunders allowing the turmoil to continue. Expressed opposition to the Iraq invasion. Blames Israel and the US for the creation of ISIS; the Yinon Plan for the refugee crisis. Opposed the polarization from the former Soviet bloc and the NATO induced isolation of Russia, but supports Ukraine without reservations. Distrust of China with worries about its new militant nationalism, the resulting decline of Western influence in Africa, especially with regards to minerals extraction, pollution and the like, Taiwan, South China Sea. Questions the viability of the Normalization processes with Israel. All pretty predictable. Then I had him stress a desire for more personal material wealth and embellish it with hints about needing to even a score with the established order by declaring his independence from it. Things like that."

"So," Sheldon ventured, "we're saying a classic profile of a moderately successful but unfulfilled Western businessman in a dead-end existence? Kind of reaching the end of his patience, worried about the future, or lack thereof?"

"Exactly," Lindsey answered. "A malcontent ripe for the picking."

The group was quiet. "And?" Scott eventually said.

"And we've had our first nibble."

Again, the room was hushed. Lindsey continued. "Sparrow has decided to help Kevin out. She's been encouraging him to get involved with the Xenox Corporation. She wants to introduce Kevin to Xenox himself."

Gloria shuffled her papers nervously as was her habit.

"This has been simmering for some time and just recently has come to a boil. I have been stalling since up to now there has been no indication of urgency or even a reason to make the move." Lindsey stood and stretched, then sat again. "This is a slim opportunity," he said almost apologetically. "But it seems to be about all we have."

"What about California?" Scott asked.

"Well, we're still onto that end as well, but as far as I can tell, it's all production out there. We've got a man keeping a close eye on the situation. He reports in regularly, but even he hasn't a clue about this. Nor do his superiors, the ones who recruited him," he added with emphasis. "They still think it's all just about vibration detection meters and making huge profits. Whatever central control that may exist to set off any or all of these devices must be focused on the man Xenox. It's the only scenario that corresponds with any kind of logical causal sense. If there's a pivotal nerve center, a computer, a code, a button, whatever, it must be linked to Xenox."

"And Kevin has to ..." Scott began.

"Find it and destroy it." Sheldon finished.

"Seek and destroy," Lindsey agreed. "We have no options."

The conference had ended but its participants were still in too great a state of shock to leave.

Lindsey added an afterthought. "I needn't have to remind you to maintain absolute secrecy. I won't be able to keep this from the White House. But we need airtight security on our end. Leaks are not conceivable, and if I can keep this between the President and myself for now, I certainly will." As an afterthought he prayed silently "and no tweets or twitters."

The trance was broken. Lindsey remained seated but the others wearily rose to leave. "Keep your cell phones close." Scott, Sheldon and Gloria nodded and shuffled out the door. Lindsey sat alone for a moment, caught a familiar glimpse of his reflection in the window, stared at it without recognition, then he too stood up and walked determinedly from the room.

- - -

The lights glittered on the polished surface of the conference table in the deserted room before dimming to orange. Before winking out completely the door opened and they automatically flared bright again. The janitor in blue coveralls entered, sprayed the table and dusted it with a yellow cloth. He straightened the chairs and unclipped his ballpoint pen digital recording device. He passed it like a wand under the table, performed his data recorded verification checks, made sure the recorder was clean and empty, and unhurriedly left the room. The momentarily violated hush returned serenely as the lights dimmed and switched off.

(68)

The man in the dark blue coveralls walked unhesitatingly along the fluorescent glare of the corridor. He ducked into a service elevator and rode it directly to the janitor locker room in an upper basement. There were other more sinister lower levels but the service lift stopped here. He stripped off his work uniform and slipped into street clothes. He reached into his coverall pocket and retrieved his pen. He slid it into his breast shirt pocket and began to whistle softly stopping briefly to comb his hair and wash his hands. He dabbed water on his face then pushed through the door into the hallway just as two other men in blue barged in.

"Hey Roger," one called "Have a good weekend."

"Back at you," Roger answered.

He walked up a carpeted concrete incline and stopped at a security checkpoint. He reached for his wallet, keys, Swiss Army knife and ball point pen and dropped them into a hard-plastic tray. He stepped through the scanner. There was no bleep.

"Night Charlie," he said to the night watchman sitting with book in hand and one eye on a digital monitor screen.

Charlie passed him the tray with barely a glance. Roger continued confidently out the exit and stepped into the brisk Virginia night air. Low clouds hung dark and threatening overhead. A storm was brewing.

- - -

The pre-millennium Ford Explorer SUV accelerated into the sparsely flowing turnpike traffic. It was enveloped in an opaque cloud of shadow and veiled in sleet. Roger flipped the cover off an instrument panel and inserted his ballpoint recorder into a circular receptacle. He gave it a twist to activate it, then pressed a "play" button.

- - -

The muffled sound of chairs scuffling on carpet and the sighs of shuffling feet came clearly over the vehicle's stereo speakers. There were sitting noises and the ruffle of paper.

Lindsey coughed. "Thanks for convening at this hour. Kevin Varyte called from London," he checked his watch, "less than three hours ago." His voice faltered. "The Xenox matter…" he began but his words trailed off.

Other voices picked up and mingled questioningly. Overlapping each other, Sheldon Rynders, Scott Freeman and Gloria Lang-Anker all tried to speak at once. "Xenox? And Kevin. Oh yes. More News? I thought we'd pretty much buried that case. Not much there, I think. Wasn't it traffic meters or something? Vibration boxes? Meters? Big bucks from what I recall."

Lindsey's voice was controlled but barely audible, a dry whisper. "They, they … "

There was an immediate uneasy silence. "They are bombs. High explosives."

The other voices gasped simultaneously. "What? How? Impossible!"

Lindsey cut in. "Plastic explosives, ultra-powerful cyclonite. Some special mixture they identified at our lab in London. That is what Sparrow was doing in Libya. The battery packs, the part that we missed when California got ahold of that meter from the warehouse operation out in Ventura. The part that the lab boys here jerry-rigged for our demonstration some six months ago.

The battery vibration detector package, well we simply guessed what components would have to be in them to fit inside the whole apparatus. And now we've discovered they are not only part battery to operate the meters but they also contain blocks of this high-grade cyclonite mixture. An electrical impulse, a coded signal, or any transmission could set off a detonator which would blow the whole box and whatever it may be attached to, to smithereens. If they are interconnected in some kind of electronic series ..." He didn't need to finish.

"Is there enough product in each meter to do major damage?" Scott asked.

"We believe so," Lindsey answered. "Given the dimensions and the apparent mixture of ingredients, we're almost certain each one has the capability of decommissioning if not demolishing any structure it may be fastened to. In the event of coordinated blasts, there may be harmonic pulsation issues that we can't even calculate."

"Freeway support poles," Gloria said shakily.

"Bridges," Sheldon added.

"Among many, many, many other things," Lindsey concluded.

- - -

The automobile stereo speakers filled with silence. A laden semi rumbled by Roger's SUV rocking it with a wash of dirty slush and flooding the cab with a torrent of blinding lights. It jammed on its engine Jake brakes in a string of obnoxious blasts and sidled off onto an exit ramp.

A lighter flicked in the playback stillness, then snapped shut. There was a sound of inhaling. "My God," Sheldon's voice stammered. "What are we going to do?" Papers rustled.

"We have miscalculated the true circumstances," Gloria's voice said hesitantly.

"No kidding," Sheldon exclaimed. "No friggin' kidding! It's been well over six months since this operation went into full swing. They'll have every major bridge, freeway overpass, tunnel or whatever in every city in the country ..."

- - -

Misshapen clouds of icy smoke blew heavily against the windscreen as Roger drove carefully through the erratic weather. The vehicle shuddered with gusts that came first from one side then the other as his night's commute groaned steadily on. Around him other headlights lost within their own precious worlds streamed homewards through the melee hopeful for warmth and comfort. Roger slowed, signaled his exit and coasted down a ramp to stop at a deserted crosswalk red light. The steady drizzle of freezing rain showed no sign of letting up.

- - -

Lindsey's voice sounded ethereal against the ice crusted scrape of the windscreen wipers. "... and if I can keep this between the President and myself for now, I certainly will." There was a pause followed by shuffling noises "Keep your cell phones close."

The red light turned green. Roger carefully accelerated through the intersection. The recorded sounds of departure signaled the end of the conference. Roger hit "rewind" for an instant, then "play" again, "... control that may exist to set any or all of these devices off must be focused on the man Xenox. It's the only scenario that corresponds with any kind of logical causal sense. If there's a pivotal nerve center, a computer, a code, a button, whatever, it must be linked to Xenox."

"And Kevin has to …"

"Find it and destroy it."

"Seek and destroy. We have no options."

- - -

Roger removed his pen device and slipped it safely into his pocket. He gazed at the weather conditions for a moment and sighed. He tapped a string of numbers on his cell phone.

An indistinguishable voice answered, "Roger?"

"Yeah. I believe our anticipated problem has occurred," he replied. "We're at Stage Two."

(69)

The Bombardier Lear Jet 85 banked gently around the glittering lights of New York City in a wide circle after traveling south along the coastline. Surrendering altitude to a slowing speed, it descended northward along Long Island towards its destination at Xenox Corporation's executive airpark. Kevin was the sole passenger on board. He had received a call in London from Lindsey Merrick three days earlier giving him a green light. He had immediately contacted Chloe in Geneva. This meeting had been anticipated for some weeks and Chloe as expected had had no problems arranging it.

The logistics were simple. Two anxious days later he met a Xenox company pilot at an executive terminal at Gatwick and within an hour found himself comfortably, if a bit nervously, winging west. The dark grey jet with its bold red Xenox logo chased the setting sun across the North Atlantic taking the Europe-America sky highway over Greenland, crossing Newfoundland and Labrador and skirting the Nova Scotia shores.

The shudder of airbrakes shook the cabin momentarily. The seat belt light flicked on and the pilot's voice announced over the intercom, "We will be landing in just a few moments, Mr. Josephs." The landing gear unfolded with a barely perceptible jolt. Kevin buckled his seatbelt as the plane approached the landing field tarmac. The glowing yellow and phosphorous blue runway lights rushed up to greet them. The plane touched gently down.

The plane taxied and lurched to a halt by a well-lit hanger sporting another red Xenox logo. Kevin could see a dark luxury sedan waiting in the bright lights. The stairway unfolded smoothly. The pilot opened the cockpit door and glanced back at Kevin. "Here we are. Hope the flight was okay for you. Welcome to Xenox America." Kevin thanked him as he stooped through the doorway and descended the steps carrying his compact travel bag.

He heard a familiar and welcome voice calling from the car. "Chris, over here!" Kevin trotted over and ducked into the back seat. "I've missed you Christopher," Chloe cooed as the door shut and the vehicle eased forward.

Kevin embraced her warmly and gave her a lingering kiss. "Likewise," he answered. "Well, here I am. This is it then? The time and place to meet your boss, the kingpin, Mr. Big, Xenox himself at long last."

"He is looking forward to meeting you," Chloe said reassuringly. "He hopes you will be a challenge."

"I'll try not to disappoint him," Kevin responded reassuringly with a wink.

It was a short drive and the two snuggled comfortably with each other. There was not much more that needed to be said. "How was the flight?"

"Great, of course. I've never flown in such private luxury."

"I usually travel by commercial myself," Chloe said. "The jet just happened to be in the right place at the right time for you."

The sedan passed through a guarded gate that automatically opened as they approached. Kevin could distinguish a spot lit red brick mansion partially hidden behind a row of silhouetted oak trees and high hedges. A fog lay on the grass and the surrounding night was lost in shadows. Few stars were visible.

(70)

A man in a maroon servant's uniform pushed open a heavy ornate door and ushered a refreshed Kevin into a spacious dining room. He had had time for a shower and change of clothes in his room. He glanced around himself. An elegant chandelier hung elaborately over the center of a great oak table on which silver serving bowls sat on embroidered mats. Chloe sparkled at one side of the table. Three other chairs were empty.

The servant walked to the vacant chair across from the girl, pulled it out and waited for Kevin to seat himself. Chloe smiled from the other side of a ceramic vase of deep red roses. She remained silent while the servant returned to the door and exited. Kevin took the moment to take in his surroundings. Bone China plates were lined with gold ornamentation. The old English style cutlery seemed to be actual gold. He picked up a fork which had the heavy luxurious feel of 24 Karats. The table had been shortened for the evening's small seating, but it was obvious that it could be extended for more formal functions. Long velvet curtains tastefully bordered floor to ceiling windows along the length of an outer wall. Behind the head of the table a massive granite fireplace dominated the darkness at the far reach of the hall. Numerous flags of various countries hung from the walls on either side of the central hearth. Kevin was studying them when the door closed behind the exiting servant.

"Mr. Xenox's flag collection," Chloe said. "Or part of it." Before she had time to elaborate, the door opened again and Xenox entered. He was accompanied by another thinner man, two men to fill the two vacant seats.

Kevin's first impression of Xenox was of solidity. The man was heavy, obviously overweight and well plied with creature comforts, but he carried himself with an earthy sturdiness that belied a cushy existence. The classic strength and durability of the Mediterranean peasantry radiated through this façade, but Kevin was quick to recognize a disquieting vein of ruthless ambition common to those who were born to lower circumstances. From what Chloe had told him of the man, Kevin was not surprised by Xenox's appearance. Still, he shivered involuntarily. An insatiable hunger for power, and then more power lurked beneath a placid veneer. It was disturbing. He shifted his attention to the tall man next to Xenox.

Kevin recognized the man, Redlinger, from the descriptive dossier Lindsey had sent him. The Xenox Corporation file was comprehensive. Redlinger had been labeled as an instigator. The word was aptly fitting.

"Ah. Chloe, Miss Tanyas," Xenox spoke as he approached the table. The servant was ahead of him to pull out his chair. Kevin rose but was waved to remain sitting. "No, no please," he said. Xenox sat comfortably. Redlinger seated himself at the opposite end of the table. "So, this is your interesting friend Mr. –".

Chloe jumped in to fill the pause. "Xandrieu, this is Christopher Josephs, trader in industrial precious and rare-earth metals."

"Yes, Mr. Josephs," Xenox continued. He studied Kevin carefully. "Chloe has impressed me with your unique qualifications and experience. You seem to be an interesting product of our times."

"Chloe has presented yourself as a greatly more interesting man," Kevin responded gracefully. Xenox grinned and bowed his head slightly.

A crew of waiters descended on the small party bringing all manner of delicacies that Kevin was not quite familiar with. He assumed correctly that they were mostly Mediterranean. The conversation turned directly to the excellent cuisine and remained complimentary well into the main courses.

Kevin eventually felt compelled to comment on the mansion itself, the dining room, the great fireplace, made from Rocky Mountain stone he learned. "I was noticing the many flags you have hanging," he ventured.

Xenox chuckled. Kevin found the man charming and deceptively disarming. He reminded himself that a chuckling man usually does so in his own interests, which could mean anything, good or evil, for those around him.

"In my philosophy," Xenox stated, "I find flags most embarrassing." He indicated the wall with a sweeping motion. "That is why I collect them, I suppose. They are so, how do you say, so archaic. How do you feel, Mr. Josephs?"

Kevin was pensive for a moment. "I haven't really given in much thought," he said. "But actually, they do seem sort of ..." He paused trying to choose the right word. "Well, sort of hypocritical."

Xenox laughed out loud. "Hypocritical, hypocritical. Excellent Mr. Josephs, excellent."

Kevin smiled. Right word, he thought.

Xenox toasted the table in general with a nearly empty glass of red wine. A waiter hurried to fill it. He continued pleased with his guest, "I mean honestly, what is a nation today? Or for that matter, what has a nation ever been throughout history? Nothing. Nothing but a collection of people led by a collection of leaders called a government which is in turn led by a collection of business and trade interests lead by international banks. All directed by an invisible hand of necessity, the mother of invention - economics."

Kevin quickly accepted his role and fell in with the game, playing dumb. He never found cause to overstep his hosts. His profession called for a mindset devoid of political opinions. Opinions are for policy makers, not intelligence gatherers. "You wouldn't say that government controls business then?" he asked innocently.

"Ha Ha Ha, Mr. Josephs," Xenox laughed jovially. "You are indeed an interesting fellow. What a sense of humour he has." He winked at Chloe and continued, "These governments, or whatever you want to call them, they try to appear to be in control and all the world's business interests do their very best to give the outward impression of being under government control. Billions of dollars are wasted in the efforts without a doubt, but it is all a sham, a theatrical farce. It's an elaborate game of charades as they used to call it, a horse drawn traveling medicine show play. There's a never-ending supply of creatures to buy into the illusion. Therein lays the beauty and magic of it all, no one can do anything about it. Even if someone becomes aware or just suspects this skullduggery exists, who wants to know? Who wants that kind of responsibility? No one, of course. So naturally it is simply passed along to conspiracy theorists and everyone else wash their hands and themselves from the stigma of suspicions. No, Mr. Josephs, it is the economic forces that are in control and they flow like flood waters around every obstacle placed in their way."

"But the people elect their own leaders," Chloe put in, "at least in the free democracies."

Xenox corrected her as if she were a school girl or his daughter. "Free democracies?" he rubbed his chin in mock perplexity as if deep in thought. "Oh, you mean voters, that less than twenty percent of the famous ninety-nine percent we hear so much about. Well, the closest thing that those people can vote for is an image. And who hands or sells them their images to choose from?"

"Business," Kevin said dryly, "Economic forces."

"Ah, you pretend not to understand, but you learn quickly. I think you are wise, Mr. Josephs. It is all economics. And a bit of greed, naturally, and power," he said innocently. "If there is money, profit in any way means or form to be made be sure that it will be made." He paused and then added absently in an ominously tinged tone, "in any way, means or form."

He continued, "The haves will continue to have, and to keep, and those who have-not, will continue to have-not unless circumstances favor those who have to allow those who have-not to have." He snorted slightly at his own semantic humor.

Kevin sorted it out. "Couldn't that be considered rather simplified?" he asked carefully.

"Mr. Xenox runs all his enterprises as simply as possible," Redlinger, quiet until now, said in an unfriendly drawl. "You see, it is most effective that way."

"Yes, truth," Xenox reflected glossing over Redlinger's gruff manner "is the simplest thing in existence. The more complicated a matter is made, the further it drifts from truth. The fact is that no matter how talented or even aggressive an individual may be, if the people holding the reins, the haves, those is power, for some reason do not want this individual around, he or she may as well just forget their ambitions. Some people are just born for acceptance. Perhaps it's a quality of unawareness or reflexive conformity that they inherit, while others often very talented souls are left out in the cold or must search for a more accepting society. Could be religious differences, too. After all religions are really self-sustaining herds of like-minded people – like governments. It is a strange meta-physical phenomenon which seems to control the casting of life's characters. I have little doubt it exists. Witness my own humble life."

Kevin glanced about himself. "Humble indeed," he commented. "So where are we in this great farce now?"

Xenox grinned. "Imagine a seesaw. The haves and have-nots are at either end. And in the middle is the vast fulcrum, the mind-numbing middle class, or what's left of it," he chortled. "Those who read the daily papers and religiously watch the television, and actually believe all that is said about the very rich and the very poor, the haves and have-nots, both who neither bother to watch or listen to much of anything to begin with." He paused contemplatively.

"Now myself, when my family came to America, we were outsiders, ethnically and economically. I was even an outsider to my own family," he shrugged. "Ah well, so be it. Some of us accepted the roles we were handed, or allowed I should say, and were consequently buried in society. Not for me. I wrote my own role and rules."

"But you are one of the great 'haves' now of course?" Kevin added.

"Of course, of course," Xenox waved his arm at the wealth surrounding him. "I wanted what I was not allowed to want, so I had to take it in my own way. It was not handed to me, but I knew it was mine. And so ..."

"And so," Kevin repeated.

"To make a long story short, eventually I had to be accepted. I was too good of an opportunity. I became good business, an asset. Basic economics again, you see."

"That leaves us 'have-nots' in a rather difficult predicament it seems," Kevin observed wryly.

Xenox grinned. "Ah yes, I'm afraid so. But who is to say? Power, that is what it's really all about."

"Power and economics," Redlinger all but growled.

Xenox turned with a vacant stare at his lieutenant. "Yes," he sighed wearily as if reminded by this unimaginative man that all his philosophizing was, in actuality, sadly true. "Power and economics." He reached for a pronged ball shaped bell and gave it a shake. "Enough of this dismal talk let us retire to the sitting room."

Redlinger stood and excused himself. "I must return to the city," he said gruffly.

"Yes, yes," his boss agreed. "Business first naturally."

Redlinger strutted to the door as the waiters cleared the table. The remaining three walked towards a smaller ornate door on one side of the hearth. "See what I must contend with?" Xenox shrugged. "Business, always business." He grinned. "Alas, it is the fate of the 'haves' and the only way to keep our seats on the seesaw."

(71)

The lounge radiated the warm glow of an open fire. The smaller hearth was built directly behind the grand stone fireplace of the dining room so that both shared the same chimney. Various flags draped the walls of this room as well. Plush sitting chairs faced the fire. An immaculate polar bear rug lay scowling its glassy stare over a polished mahogany floor.

Kevin took a seat nearest the fire. Chloe curled herself nearby on the snowy fur. Xenox retired into the shadows to retrieve brandy and glasses. He poured generously, passed the delicate crystal vessels around and took a place himself.

"About this business of flags," he said looking around the room. "I imagine you have difficulty associating with any one in particular, Mr. Josephs? An American living many years in Europe, hopping between London, Paris, Geneva, etcetera, commuting to all parts of the globe, rarely in the United States except on business, and then only briefly. I would think that could make one ponder where one's loyalties lie precisely?"

Kevin uttered a noncommittal sound between sips of brandy.

"Or have you sided with Her Majesty?" Xenox asked amused. "For Queen, or King now, I should say, and country and all that rot that most Americans find so seductive?" He opened an elaborately carved yellow wooden box. "From the old Yugoslav countryside." He offered a cigar to Kevin. "From Havana, of course."

"Of course," Kevin smiled, taking one.

Xenox took another and snipped an end off each with an ornate silver clipper. "From Scandinavia." He took an ember from the fire with slender iron tongs. "From England." And lit both cigars with it.

Kevin inhaled shallowly. He rarely smoked these days, and when he did, he avoided sucking the nicotine deep into his lungs as is the habit of diehard heavy smokers. Xenox inhaled moderately savoring the tobacco.

"Well," Kevin ventured. "I do find the British lifestyle and attitudes very, uh, comforting."

"I find it rather perverse myself," Xenox stated flatly. "London, I'm sure, will look extraordinarily inviting to, say, someone from Iraq or Pakistan or India, or from anywhere in the old colonial empire, actually; or even from my old country – "

"Greece?" Kevin interrupted.

"Yes, Greece," Xenox nodded. "But the modern countries of Europe, France Germany, Denmark, and all, find the island slightly obscene." He was thoughtful for a moment. "And vice versa of course," he added humorously. "But never mind. So why the American fascination I wonder?"

Kevin was noncommittal. He did not revel in these types of discussions. "Strange, isn't it?"

"I prefer perverse," Xenox persisted. "The two governments, America and England, keep a polite distance, held together by mutual distrust and a common language. But then all governments behave the same to each other regardless, I suppose."

"Probably," Kevin agreed.

"Without a doubt. They all know the same secrets of governing. It must be extremely embarrassing to face foreigners doing to their people what you are doing to your own. It makes them almost equals and that goes beyond embarrassing to discomfort; in a simplified scenario, of course."

"Of course," Kevin nodded and toasted with his glass.

"So, we keep our distances, these nations. It is more comfortable and one minimizes the need to squirm." Xenox smirked.

"A bit like the way corporations treat each other," Kevin noted casually.

Xenox guffawed. "You make me laugh Mr. Josephs. That is a good quality in a man. Yes, like corporations; it's business and trade." He made the universal fingers and thumb gesture for money. "Every organization out for its own profit doing whatever it can get away with, filled naturally with individuals doing whatever they can get away with to get as much as they can. It's a perfect system."

"Doing what they can get away with?" Kevin wrinkled his brow.

"Exactly, like me, like you, like all of us. We all push the envelope in our own favour. Some are a little more zealous than others, it's true, but we have to maximize our advantage, mustn't we?"

"I suppose so," Kevin agreed reluctantly.

"Sure. We cut corners to make a little more from a little less. It's nothing to be ashamed of. If we don't, someone else will."

Kevin thought for a moment. "And the quality of life?"

"Ah yes, the quality of life. What does that mean? More money and wealth, from all I can tell," Xenox continued. "Take the farmers in Qingyuan, China as an example. They found their idyllic agricultural landscape transformed into a polluted city of nearly four million people in less than a single generation. All kinds of health problems came with it, respiratory disease, cancer, you name it, but they now have comfortable apartments, cars, new TVs, all kinds of electronic gadgets. Did their quality of life, as you say, go up or down?"

Kevin shrugged.

"That's right. Who's to judge? Ask the average Ling Lu if he would rather be breaking his back for subsistence wages in clean rice fields or rolling in filthy import-export wealth. No one wants to go backwards, even if the air they breathe is now so foul it can be tasted with a spoon. It is the fulcrum of the seesaw, the great public, Marx's masses; these are the ones who suffer. But such is life."

"Such is life," Kevin repeated as if trying on a new suit, vaguely attentive and fingering the fabric.

"Yes, yes. Such is life," Xenox emphasized, the salesman with a "this suit is you, sir" attitude. "But if life quality declines too much, and trade breaks down, well, we can always go to war over some pretext."

"Now war?" Kevin thought to himself. "War?" he said surprised.

"War, the only time we really get up close and personal with our enemies, those who may have been our dearest friends ten years before. Then we can afford to see both sides and see each other as one and the same, but at opposite ends of gun barrels. Perhaps it's because everyone wants the same things but we all can't have them. Then when it's all too late, we cry out 'why are we fighting?'".

Chloe gazed into the fire savoring only the moment and the brandy. Kevin watched her. "It does seem kind of pointless," he agreed.

"Yes, and nowadays even winning a war is an obsolete concept, impossible so to speak. No side can win in a nuclear showdown, as every school child knows. So, the strife is kept minimized, in a maximized sort of way, which means, at least, localized and, may I say, prolonged."

"Prolonged?"

"Yes, yes, of course. The longer a conflict goes on the more profit we make. It's lovely. Just keep the unfortunate collateral carnage contained and far from the public eye and the money keeps rolling in. The Iran-Iraq War," he said almost gleefully, "everybody won there, except the people fighting it. Afghanistan and Iraq? - textbook. Israel-Palestine, pure genius - America hands over its sovereignty and wealth to a repressive and now, apartheid, foreign country whose citizens and army even kill Americans, and the common Joe Blow on Main Street, USA violently defends doing so." He cut short a brief laugh.

"True," Kevin had to admit. Xenox was historically accurate.

"It used to be that, sadly, these conflicts would come to an end and others would have to be invented. But today? Not today, oh no. Today the war is happily forever, just like that bloody old English drunk Orwell predicted. Endless war to keep the fabric of society together. Ironic, but lovely, I can't think of a better word. Just lovely," Xenox beamed. "War forever."

"And minimized?" Kevin questioned. "Surely today's Middle East conflicts aren't minimized."

"Oh, but they are," Xenox continued. "Has anyone dropped an atomic warhead, except maybe a single small one or two in, say, Yemen? Obviously, not. A nuclear outbreak would mean total destruction; destruction of life, liberty, property and even tyranny. Who wants that?"

"But it can happen?"

"No one knows. That's the beauty of it. That's why it exists. It's the great unknown, the threat, the possibility that hangs over us, blackmailing us all. It keeps the armament race going. It turns our friends to foes and foes to friends continuously like cosmic clockwork. It makes a nation truly believe it can dominate all others and be on top forever. When the Soviet Union crumbled, the West gloated instead of grabbing the reigns and the opportunity to economically tame the great evil ex-empire. The West wallowed in its own false glory and went on to make all the same mistakes the East did earlier. Time runs out and is squandered by these ignorant governments. Look at Afghanistan now, as America attempted to slither away covering up any remorse or responsibility in the dead of night. What nonsense. What beautiful, but self-destructive, corruption. And in Iraq? They easily succumbed to their politically retarded shortsighted efforts. And are still at it in Syria."

"Now Russia thinks it can dominate again, first by conquering Ukraine and threatening nuclear holocaust for all, while America has been trying to retreat, unsuccessfully, I might add, into itself like a clam. A new Cold War is in progress, totally unnecessary and completely pointless. Brilliant. China pushes its boundaries and its economic grip into the Third World on its peripheries and Africa, which conveniently festers and implodes internally from time to time. The migrants in Europe have done their best at cultural disruption, intentionally or not. Oh, it goes on and on, but no nuclear explosions, so far. God willing." Xenox sighed deeply. "What can anyone do?" He toasted the air. "Build another wall?"

"Disarm?" Kevin suggested.

"Peace?" Xenox asked with skepticism. "Too simple, too easy, too impossible. No one trusts anyone else, how can there be peace? No, our situation 'is', and cannot change or be doubted. We must fight each other, without 'us' actually doing the fighting, of course," he grinned. "On a global scale, we keep things limited with, so far, no nuclear devices going off. It's fairly hopeless, but not worth worrying about unless you're a 'leader' so to speak."

"So, what's the purpose?" Kevin wondered.

"To win, Christopher, always to win," Xenox answered prophetically, solemnly adding, "Winning isn't everything, it's the only thing, you see, even when winning is statistically impossible."

[72]

Kevin sauntered down a curving black marble staircase that sparkled in the clear morning sunlight. Pale silk curtains gleamed casting a veiled fluorescent glow around the Xenox mansion entrance hallway. Chloe waited at the bottom dressed in an informal beige suit.

"Sleep well?" she asked as Kevin approached.

He grinned. "Well, and satisfied after I left your room."

Chloe smirked. "Shall we have breakfast?"

"After you, M' lady." Kevin held out his arm and escorted Chole formally into the dining hall.

The drapes were drawn wide and a window partially opened. The great room flittered in clean air and dazzling sunshine. It was a startling change from the heaviness of the night before. A breeze ruffled the flags nearest the tall windows.

Xandrieu Xenox was cheerfully polishing off a plate of scrambled eggs, bacon, toast and marmalade. He took a gulp of fresh brewed coffee. "Come in. Come in," he beamed as the couple entered.

"Good morning," the two chimed simultaneously, Chloe's voice lingering a formal "Sir." They took seats opposite Xenox. A servant dressed in white poured coffee and took their order preferences.

Xenox began immediately. "Chloe tells me you are dissatisfied with your work," he said, cryptically adding "And many things."

Kevin was direct and matter-of-fact, "Yes."

Xenox lifted an eyebrow waiting for an elaboration that didn't come. He continued, "You disagree with your home government's policies. But that is rather common, I would think. But specifically, you have issues internationally, in for instance the Middle East. Why?"

Kevin took a swig of hot black coffee from a spotless white China cup. "The Middle East is a large area," he responded carefully, prudently adding, "Sir."

Xenox chuckled. "Israel, for starters. It seems to be quite a polarizing subject," he said flatly. "It's a litmus paper that tends to give an idea on what side of many things one is willing to stand with."

"I have learned to sympathize with the Palestinians," Kevin admitted.

"And why is that?"

"Many reasons. I think they deserve more," Kevin responded, playing coy. The waiter placed two over-medium fried eggs with crispy ham and fluffy biscuits before him. Chloe had scrambled and bacon, like her boss.

"More?" Xenox probed.

"They deserve a fighting chance, their own homeland, like the Israelis," Kevin replied falling headlong into his role. "There's no point going into all the details. I'm sure you already know how unfairly they've been treated." Xenox nodded. "The problem is that so many people don't know, and have essentially been hoodwinked by mainstream media outlets or manipulated by political-religious powers into blindly supporting one side, Israel."

"That seems to be perceptively changing," Xenox noted.

"Yes, very slowly," Kevin agreed. "More information is getting out these days, but the grip of fear of being branded antisemitic is still so strong that otherwise moral people end up self-righteously supporting murder and war crimes against women, children and civilians. It's madness."

"Similar to the treatment doled out to your indigenous Indians?"

Kevin paused. "Yes, that's true. The analogy has been used quite often to point out our own hypocrisy. Don't cast stones, they say. We, or our ancestors at least, used 'manifest destiny' as moral cover. The Zionists today use and over-use 'holocaust guilt' and claim self-defense when maiming and killing unarmed protestors. Call it what you like. It's all madness, and sets us up to be on one side or the other, US politics, no in-between. And that's not fair, or right." He concentrated on his eggs silently.

"And what do you think can be done about it? Say by your government? Deny Israel's 'right to exist'?" Xenox asked in a tone that could have been offended.

Kevin suffered a spasm of doubt. He hoped he wasn't over-acting. "No, no," he continued. "Israel has those rights, of course, but so does Palestine."

"Right to exist. What kind of an expression is that?" Xenox laughed. "Politicians should be banned from voicing the concept altogether. It's a pretense, actually. Ask a lion if a zebra has the right to exist when there is a hungry pride of cubs that need feeding."

"Yes, but we aren't animals," Kevin objected.

Xenox was thoughtful. "No, we, as individuals, aren't. But we don't survive just as individuals. Countries, corporations, businesses, most religions - we all form into mobs of varying degrees and sizes, like animals, and behave so. Nothing in my experience has shown me this is untrue. It is a lesson that should be learned young. I imagine it is what makes sports so popular, and why fans become so blood thirsty."

Kevin sighed. "Mr. Xenox, you are certainly as astute as Chloe has said. I just don't personally like supporting the injustices I see in the world today."

"Yes, yes," Mr. Josephs. "Admirable feelings." Kevin was irritated by Xenox's condescending manner. "And, your solutions?"

"Well, when you put it that way, I guess I really don't have any," Kevin answered. "Just work for peaceful coexistence, minimize injustices, educate the people, uncover the lies, and hope that future generations are smarter than we were and more able to understand how to solve problems and clean up our corrupt and polluted world. The way the world's going, they will certainly have a herculean task before them. It doesn't sound very original, I know, but that's pretty much where I am today."

"And this is enough reason for you to want to give up your line of work?"

"It's enough for me to want to get out of my own rat race and try something new and more independent."

Xenox gave his guest a long thoughtful look and laughed heartily. "Very interesting. These sentiments …" he chortled. "Impractical perhaps, but coherent; lucid and intelligent. Very, very interesting." He turned to Chloe. "You are right, my dear, I can use such a man in my organization."

Kevin breathed an imperceptible sigh of relief, and allowed himself to relax. Xenox focused his attention on Kevin. "I want you to stay close with Chloe today. You will be inspecting a few shipments and concerns in the city. Feel free to familiarize yourself with my operations. You will find I operate simply. A few trusted individuals report to me directly. I keep a small structure at top with a much broader base below, of course, since my businesses are global. A pyramid, if you will, so that the top is stable and never topples."

Kevin nodded, "Thank you, sir, for the opportunity. I will certainly take a look."

Xenox stood up, finished with his breakfast and grinned. "Do that. Do that. And don't forget to thank Miss Tanyas as well," he said encouragingly placing a hand on Kevin's shoulder. "We'll see how it goes, if it suits you, how long it might take for you to get out of your commitments, and take it from there. But now my children, I must retire to my work." He gave Chloe a kiss on the hand and left the room. Kevin and Chloe finished their breakfasts wordlessly.

- - -

In his office, Xenox sat thoughtfully gazing out an expansive window. He pressed a button and Redlinger hurried in from an adjacent room.

"You were listening to our breakfast conversation?" he asked without turning from the view.

"Of course," Redlinger answered.

Xenox nodded. "All the same, we will keep a close eye on our Mr. Christopher Josephs." Redlinger grunted an affirmation and left the office.

Below the window, a short grey limousine pulled up to the mansion's front door. Kevin and Chloe stepped inside and the automobile headed towards the estate gates. Xenox watched as the vehicle slowed at the barred entrance. The gates opened and the car sped out of sight behind a rise in the land.

Moments later, a black Mercedes with Redlinger at the wheel, repeated the procedure. Satisfied, Xenox turned back to his telephones and his papers.

[73]

Roger climbed the short flight of red brick stairs that led to his modest apartment near Georgetown University. He could have been an older student, returned to school to pick up post-graduate credits or another degree, but he wasn't. He had chosen the small flat in the transient student area to be inconspicuous. Carry a briefcase and a few books, he figured, and no one would notice him.

Two girls came giggling out of the stairwell from a basement rental. They half-bumped into Roger before looking up. Both burst out laughing and stumbled onto the dark street. Roger caught the sweet acrid smell of marijuana as the girls passed. He watched them disappear beyond the dim glow of a single street lamp. It had been years since he had partaken in even a nibble or a puff. He considered this momentarily. He heaved a sigh, but remained expressionless.

He had called in his recorded information from Langley three weeks before from his car on that icy night. The news had been received calmly without much surprise. It had been expected that the authorities would eventually figure out the reality of the StresChek vibration monitors. Luckily, their deductions had taken some time, time which gave StresChek a significant head start advantage. And now the die was cast.

It had been well over six months since the StresChek meters had started being distributed and installed. There were thousands of them already attached to freeway overpasses, bridges and a multitude of other transportation structures in most major cities around the country. If set off at any time, they could now bring vital traffic to a virtual standstill and cause unimaginable chaos nationwide.

Main arteries had been identified in conjunction with local city governments as the most urgent in need of monitoring. These were targeted as top priority. It was a slick and flawless plan. America's infamous aging infrastructure played right along with the cards being dealt. It was unanimous amongst government officials, state and federal, that essential upgrades were required and StresChek information would prove to be just the catalyst needed to get costly improvement projects rolling.

Cities and counties were licking their lips and rubbing their hands in anticipation of large government contracts, kick-backs and reelection funds. Roger reflected on the beauty and simplicity of the plan, as well as its ambitious nationwide scope. It was full of automatic checks and, he noted the irony, integral safety checks. The authorities had finally discovered the plot, but were helpless to interrupt its progression.

Roger had continued to listened in on Lindsey Merric, but there had been no surprises. As expected, all efforts were being expended on keeping the situation hushed in-house and away from the public eye. The White House had to be notified, of course, but the circle of knowledge was tight and limited to Chiefs of Staff and trusted advisors. The Langley crew was airtight.

But as for a solution, the authorities were dumbfounded. There were no terrorist contingency plans that fit this scenario. All ideas were open to discussion and laid out on the table. Alternatives were shuffled quickly and seemingly, endlessly, but every thought, every consideration was stymied. The StresChek terrorists, as they were being called, had the upper hand by far. They held the trump card – if at any moment the authorities tipped their hand and tried to physically interfere, there would be nothing stopping a blitzkrieg from occurring. The thought was sobering. The silence of helplessness was deafening.

- - -

Days passed, then a week, and again another. In an attempt to break the impasse, Lindsey Merric was ultimately compelled to counsel the chief executive that a quiet demonstration of force was critical. Roger had taken the opportunity in the lull of activity to quietly give notice, and these weeks later, he had today left his last day of work. All direct contacts now were severed.

Lindsey's show of force was muted but pointed. Police cars had shown up on scene to closely eye numerous StresChek devices in prominent places in the larger cities. Photographs were taken and care was given to show exaggerated interest in the turquoise blue boxes. Government auditors and Internal Revenue inspectors casually ruffled the StresChek offices. Some shipments of meters had been legally delayed and carefully searched on one pretext or another. Nothing was seized or confiscated and deliveries were allowed to proceed. But the signals emitted were unmistakably clear.

- - -

Roger turned the key and entered his flat, probably, he realized, for the last time. He placed a small bag of groceries on the kitchen counter.

"A cheese and veggie omelet should be a fitting last supper", he thought. His cell phone vibrated.

"Roger," he answered.

"We're going into Stage B. Come up tomorrow night."

(74)

Mon: AM – JFK international
Introduced to Sparks
Checked incoming shipments from Europe and Med.
(mostly legit – olive oil, etc.)
PM -Lunch at airport
Procedures and operations at office
Back to Base

Tues:AM – The City, Westside Dock 14
Met Doc and Abraham
Warehouse inspection, shipment loading
(Farm machinery; cover for light arms, ammunition)
PM -Boarded Madeira, lunched with Captain Reynolds
Limo to Manhattan office
Back to Base

Weds:AM -The City; Brooklyn Dock
Inspect containers to Egypt
Procedures and office
Back to Westside; procedures and office
PM -Lunch at W 51st Grill
Back to Base

Thurs:AM -The City; StresChek warehouse and office
Operations, updates – Vans, storage, maintenance
Drive out for demo installation with Baines and technical crew
PM – Late lunch with Baines

Return to Base

Fri:AM -Newark Airport, New Jersey

"They've had quite a busy week," Xenox said. "Chloe is very comprehensive." Xenox laid the report on his office desk and looked up at Redlinger.

Redlinger nodded uncommittedly. "Yes."

"Well? What do you think?"

"He's prying," Redlinger said brusquely.

Xenox studied the man and pressed an intercom button. "Hold all calls for the moment," he spoke to his secretary. "Prying?"

Redlinger stood his ground. "I'm certain of it."

"Your obvious intense dislike for the man would have nothing to do with it, I'm sure?" Xenox asked irritably.

Redlinger flushed, then turned icy. "No, sir. It hasn't."

"Good," Xenox answered bluntly. He relished watching his second-in-command squirm. The outsider, Christopher Josephs, was an obvious threat to Redlinger. Chloe would keep her place alone, but allied with a competent man, she could be dangerous.

"So," Xenox continued, followed by an uncomfortable pause. "What makes you suspect he is prying?"

"As you see," Redlinger began, gesturing at the report, "I followed them discreetly and out of sight. I let Wes keep an eye on them during lunch when I could question our office managers. I told them the line about a new man in the organization and asked for opinions and suspicions; what he looked at and what questions were asked."

"Yes, very good," Xenox answered impatiently. "And?"

"And, Doc and Abraham were immediately suspicious …"

Xenox cut him off with a wave, "Doc and Abraham are always suspicious; even of me." He laughed. "That's why I hired them."

"Yes," Redlinger agreed expressionlessly. "They were uncomfortable with Mr. Josephs' questions concerning the light arms going to Bolivia."

"As they should be."

"And," Redlinger continued, "his apparent lack of interest in the legitimate agricultural supplies."

Xenox grunted, "Arms are more glamorous."

"And, not so many questions about routine procedures and office operations, just superficial interest."

"Continue," Xenox answered soberly.

"Sparks at Kennedy gave me a pretty much identical impression about airport transactions."

Redlinger took a folded note from his pocket and read. "He is interested, then distracted, as if looking for something but doesn't know what. Asked about borderline legality issues. Mostly ignored legit concerns, custom checks and the like."

"Perhaps, he is just cautious," Xenox said.

"Perhaps," Redlinger agreed with a hint of disdain. "He did ask a lot of questions about StresChek."

"Did he now?" Xenox asked with a hint of alarm. "That shouldn't have been so interesting. Such as?"

"Technical questions - how the meters work, what happens with the collected data, can meters be remotely switched on and off, who pays for the service, is the network nationwide or just NYC – things like that."

"And this morning they are in New Jersey?"

"Yes. I called Newark and they'll keep a watch on them and report in this evening."

Xenox swiveled his chair to look out the view and said contemplatively, half to himself, "And you think he is prying, then?"

"I do," Redlinger answered tersely.

"A government man?" Xenox queried.

"That is always a possibility."

Xenox turned back to his desk and drummed his pen on a pile of papers that needed his attention. "That is always a possibility," he repeated. "Yes." He gazed at his lieutenant. "We shall see. If he is, we know how to deal with him. And Chloe?"

"No. She is the same as always."

"Good." Xenox waved Redlinger away and he left the room. As the door closed quietly behind him, Xenox spoke absently, "We shall see, Mr. Christopher Josephs. We shall see."

[75]

Flames flickered over the blackened bricks of the massive fireplace in the Xenox library. Chloe watched them through a brandy glass, licking the caked-on soot as they slithered up the chimney and fragmented into wisps of smoke. The wind was heavy but the only evidence of a tempest this deep inside the mansion was an occasional violent sucking of air over the fire. Flames leaped and died again.

"You are nervous tonight," Chloe said in answer to Kevin's pacing.

Kevin flopped next to her on the couch. "Oh, it's just that it's been over two weeks since I got here. I've seen a pretty good cross-section of Xenox's New York operations. I'm impressed. Of course. Everything you have said is true. But I have to make up my mind soon. I can't stay away forever."

"I thought you already made up your mind," Chloe said perplexed.

"Of course, I have. But I have to get out of my commitments, as you know, without drawing attention to myself. That means a bit of a bother, explanations, severances and all that nonsense. It's just getting on my nerves, all this waiting."

Chloe was reassuring. "We should know tonight."

The door opened and Xenox stepped into the room accompanied by Redlinger, who veered off towards the bar. Kevin stood to greet him.

" Ah, there you two are," Xenox began. "I have been extremely busy this week. I humbly apologize for not meeting you sooner," he said with a mock bow. "I trust Miss Tanyas has given you a comprehensive tour of our enterprises?"

"Yes sir. She certainly has," Kevin replied.

Redlinger handed Xenox a drink. Xenox sat an in extravagantly comfortable armchair while Redlinger chose a stiff chair near the coffee table. Kevin settled back onto the couch next to Chloe.

Xenox breezed through his memory. "Kennedy airport, Newark, Brooklyn and City docks, Manhattan offices." Kevin nodded. "A nice segment of my operations. So then, what do you think of it all now?"

"Quite extensive," Kevin answered. "Most impressive."

"Indeed, thank you. I believe they are myself," Xenox replied. He caught a distrustful glance from Redlinger out of the corner of his eye but ignored it. "And what of the procedures?"

"Very efficient, Kevin answered truthfully. "Simple and most effective."

Xenox grinned. "You are most flattering, Mr. Josephs. And the legalities in some cases, did they bother you?"

Kevin took a short swallow of his whiskey. "Technicalities," he answered. "Lord knows dealing with international metals, I am certainly acquainted with those."

Xenox glanced at Redlinger who was reluctantly forced to nod. "Grey areas in a world, we can say, was never really black and white?"

"My sentiments exactly," Kevin replied with a slight grin. "Adds a little colour to the drabness. Once in Africa, coming out of the Congo –"

Xenox cut him short. "Yes, yes. We all have our stories. Some are best kept to ourselves, are they not?"

Kevin felt a twinge of embarrassment. "Yes, of course, sir."

"Well, my dear Christopher Josephs," Xenox said formally. "Assuming that you are still interested, I think your qualifications and attitude meld well with the Xenox vision. I see no reasons why we can't begin proceedings to incorporate you into the international branch of my organization immediately. Business keeps growing, as you may have noticed in the StresChek department. What a boon that enterprise has proven to be. I have been in need of another top hand for some time now. Chloe's opinion of you has been quite high and I, myself, like what I have seen. Welcome."

Kevin placed his glass on the table and stood to firmly shake hands. "Thank you. Thank you, very much, Mr. Xenox," he replied humbly. "This is quite an honor, and a momentous change in my life direction. I will do my best to live up to your expectations."

"I have no doubt that you will," Xenox said. He added, as if forgetful, "Considering the nature of many of my projects, you realize, of course, that this must be a lifetime commitment?"

"Yes. I have considered and accept that," Kevin answered evenly.

"Until, if and when a time comes that yourself and Miss Tanyas no longer feel useful here, and I am able to safely let you go, with my blessings of course." He smiled at Chloe.

"Thank you, sir. I appreciate, we appreciate that very much." Kevin beamed.

"Excellent," Xenox answered cheerfully. "I propose a toast! To Christopher Josephs and success in the Xenox Empire."

Chloe smiled. Redlinger shrugged and raised his glass halfheartedly.

"And now as an inner member and trusted employee of my organization, I feel there is something of great importance I must show you."

Redlinger started, spilling his drink. "What? But -" he began.

Xenox cut him off and waved him down. "Relax, relax. I feel it is necessary."

Redlinger inhaled deeply, colour rising in his face, and grumbled something inaudible.

"As I intend to utilize Christopher immediately as a management and coordination team with Chloe, I can see no reason to delay."

He walked to the wall adjacent to the fireplace which was a floor to ceiling bookshelf stacked with ornate leather-bound books. A complete encyclopedia set filled one shelf. Xenox removed the last volume, X to Zyzzyva. The shelf hummed momentarily, receded a foot and slid sideways. A heavy metal vault door was revealed. Xenox placed his hand on a glass panel and looked into a retina scanner. The door swung soundlessly open on well-oiled hinges.

(76)

Roger eased his car to a stop under floodlights at the Xenox airfield gates just as a dark Lear jet screeched overhead and touched down on the misty tarmac. Violet-blue ground lights glowed between a copse of silhouetted trees.

"Nice timing," he murmured to himself. He had just ended his two hundred plus mile drive from D.C. He handed a plastic identification card to the guard.

The guard smiled, "Haven't seen you up here for a while," he said.

"Nope. They've got me down in D.C. polishing office seats," he laughed.

The guard scrutinized Roger's vehicle and punched the license plate numbers into his computer console. "When are you gonna get rid of this old clunker?"

Roger laughed again, "Someday, some fine day, I'm sure." He wondered uneasily where the next few hours would take him. The computer beeped verification and the barrier rose.

"Okay, then, you take care," the guard said handing back Roger's ID.

- - -

A dim hallway disappeared into darkness. Redlinger stepped forward and the motion activated a row of LED lights. The lights fluttered illuminating the passageway in a soft white glow. The floor was tiled a pale beige. The ceiling and walls, Kevin noticed, were rough concrete. The hallway was more of a tunnel than a corridor. It disappeared around a corner following a gentle downwards slope. A small electric cart sat near the door facing the glowing passage. Redlinger walked over to it, sat in the driver's seat and turned a starting lever. The cart hummed to life.

Kevin watched wordlessly. Chloe gave him a reassuring squeeze of the hand.

"Ah, yes. My little secrets," Xenox said breaking the spell. "Come, you will enjoy this, Christopher."

The trio joined Redlinger on the cart and he eased it forward down the passageway. As the cart turned the corner, Kevin heard the clunk of the vault door locking. He swallowed.

"Are we nervous, Christopher?" Xenox asked.

Kevin realized he was being carefully scrutinized. "Just awed," he answered prudently, and truthfully.

Xenox chuckled. He reached over and patted Redlinger on the shoulder. Redlinger shrugged, irritated at the gesture. Xenox chuckled again. Annoying Redlinger was a joy he relished. The electric cart purred along, left, then right, and sharply left again. Its thick rubber tires whizzed elastically on the smooth tiles. The lights dimmed behind it as it passed. The passage dipped slightly then rose again, and repeated. Kevin tried to calculate his bearings but was easily lost. The motion was nauseating and disorienting.

"We travel about a quarter of a mile in length. Depth perception and direction are masked, as you can tell," Xenox said proudly. "That makes our exact position from above quite uncertain." He added, "Just in case."

"I see what you mean," Kevin answered. "Even the sense of movement is a bit ambiguous. I can't tell if we've gone a hundred or just twenty yards."

Xenox laughed. "My intention exactly. Otherwise, I would have built an adjoining room to the library. It's just to calm my sense of intrigue, you see."

The cart glided around a sharp corner and came to a stop facing another vaulted door, the twin of the tunnel's entrance. Redlinger pushed a button on the driver's panel and the vault mechanisms whirred. A wheel turned, a gear clicked, the lock flicked open and the door swung outwards from the tunnel. A uniformed guard sat relaxed at a desk with a compact machine gun pointed at the group. Redlinger barked an order, the man stood and came briskly to attention.

"Precautions," Xenox apologized. "These days you never can tell," he added wearily.

Redlinger led the way into a brightly lit antechamber that breathed of cool, clean air-conditioning. "I must keep a relatively chill atmosphere here," Xenox explained. "As you will see, my instruments require constant humidity and temperature levels all year round."

Redlinger had passed through a revolving glass door. Xenox, Chloe and Kevin followed him into a spacious chamber. "Pressurization keeps all dust and contaminants out," Xenox continued. "There is a slight but continuous flow of air outwards that protects the delicacies of my modern computer equipment."

Kevin was awed into silence. They were standing on a metal railed viewing platform overlooking an auditorium with several rows of computer consoles, electronic screen workstations and numerous instrument panels with glowing meters and dials. Central to the room, a large screen map of the world dominated what appeared to be Xenox's control center. Redlinger was already descending the final row of stairs, talking with a comfortably dressed technician.

Kevin's immediate impression was of a mission control room at NASA headquarters in Houston or even a SpaceX complex at Boca Chica outside of Brownsville in Texas. Maybe a dozen technicians were at various stations around the room. Another guard slowly paced the aisle armed with the signature machine pistol, a blue uniformed carbon copy of the doorway sentry. Kevin was startled to feel Chloe tugging at his sleeve.

"Come, Christopher," Xenox was saying. "We can't stay here all night."

"What?" Kevin responded snapping out of his daze. "Oh, yes. Excuse me I just – "

Xenox grinned. "I understand completely." He led the way down the stairs and crossed a grilled walkway into the control center. Below their feet, Kevin could see a complex array of wires, a spectrum of all colours and sizes, neatly tied in bundles like lengthy papyrus reeds, forking off in different directions. Uniform blue and grey, presumably lithium battery power source cabinets lined the corridor. Kevin paused to look at a pair of large circular grills about six feet in diameter.

"Exhaust vents for the pressurization system," Chloe said nudging him forward.

The guard had fallen in step a few paces behind them. He seemed banal and detached but kept a wary eye on the visitors. Xenox entered the open central area and was warmly greeted by a technician, the man Redlinger had been talking with moments before. Kevin glanced back at the air vents briefly. Behind the grills heavy fans rotated at a crisp, steady pace.

- - -

Roger drove directly to the airfield control tower. The executive jet was parked, engines steaming in the night's chill. A fuel truck was parked next to it. The driver had the plane safely grounded to protect from static sparking and was diligently refueling the glistening machine. Roger stopped his car and got out. He stood by his old Ford Explorer and patted his tattered friend on the hood. "I'll miss you," he sighed. "Thanks."

He gazed at the cloudless sky, the stars and a hazy urban glow from the city beyond, and entered the tower. "Hey, Tom," he said to the pilot who lounged comfortably with a hot cup of coffee.

"Hey, Rog," Tom answered. He glanced up the stairs and indicated with his eyebrows.

Roger followed the glance and nodded. "Uh, huh. See you in a few."

A man stood alone in darkness gazing at the lights outside the windows. Inside, instruments glowed warmly, reds and greens with touches of blue reflected on the panes. Outside, blue airfield lights tinted the ground mixing with the glow of scattered yellow and red lanterns. Stars hung low on the visible horizon above the trees. He was tall, dressed casually in a suede jacket, jeans and dark boots. Except for his height, he could easily blend in with any crowd. He turned to a monitor screen that had been warming up and now produced a clear black and white picture. His face was bathed in a pale light. He fiddled with the controls searching the closed-circuit camera network of the Xenox mansion and property. The scene he was looking for materialized.

Roger reached the top of the stairs and opened the door. Without turning, the man greeted him. "Hello, Roger. What do you have?"

"Nothing new. It is confirmed that this Christopher Josephs is definitely Kevin Varyte, US intelligence, as we assumed. No surprise there."

The man turned towards him. "I see, then as I suspected we have little time to lose. Look here."

Roger walked over to the monitor. He could see Kevin and Chloe moving forward along a walkway followed by an armed guard. Kevin looked over his shoulder at what appeared to be air vents. "He's gotten further than I would have thought," Roger commented.

"Yes," Hank Bellard said. "Xenox seems to be quite taken with him." He reached for a land line telephone with a row of buttons connecting a myriad of lines to the one handset. He punched a number and waited.

(77)

At a White House communications switchboard, a night operator answered the buzz. "The White House," he said simply.

A voice at the other end said, "I must speak with the President."

The aide rolled his eyes to the heavens, and sighed. "Not another one," he groaned and switched into his automatic response. "I'm sorry, sir. That is out of the question. The President can only be con –". He was cut short.

"Just mention StresChek."

The aide glanced nervously at a special memo that had been posted on the wall for the past several days. "One moment, sir," he answered.

[78]

"And so," Xenox said proudly waving his arm when Kevin and Chloe caught up with him at a large panel. "My command center."

"Incredible," Kevin praised. Chloe was quietly awed as always when she came into this chamber, which was seldom.

"As we have discussed, some of my activities are not, as one could say, strictly legitimate, not precisely legal, that is depending on your point of view, or on which government, or even government agency, you happen to support." Xenox gave Kevin a sidelong glance, saw no reaction and continued, satisfied.

"Let's take the Arabian Gulf, or should I say Persian Gulf?" He indicated the electronic world map that dominated the central wall and zoomed the view in towards it.

"It's all a matter of point of view, again," Kevin answered slyly.

"Quite so, Christopher. So, shall we be neutral? The Gulf, then." Xenox pressed a button. A pin prick blue light popped out brightly in the middle of the salty warm waters of the oil rich Gulf. "This blue light, here. Let us imagine that it signifies a moderately-sized oil tanker, leased, of course, to the Xenox Worldwide Corporation. And let us say, it is bound for Kharg Island in Iranian claimed waters." He pressed another button and a white light shone on indicating the Iranian refinery and oil terminal island.

Redlinger was huddled with an engineer, removed from the little demonstration and seemingly uninterested. But one eye constantly wandered towards Christopher Josephs, suspiciously seeking telltale signs of an ulterior motive, changes in facial expressions, sudden reactions. There were none, so far. He kept his distance like an alert Doberman Pincer.

Xenox pressed another button. A red light flickered on not far from the blue blip. "And this red light? We'll have it representing the Iranian Navy, a frigate class destroyer."

Kevin nodded.

"Now, let us suppose our tanker, our blue light, is empty," he paused. "At least, empty of oil, that is. And, if we really stretch our imagination, we can visualize that the tanker's hold carries, not oil as it should according to its shipping manifests and documents, but an array of long-range missile launchers, explosives, light artillery and other such amusing toys."

Xenox regarded Mr. Josephs. Kevin's eye twitched, but he showed no other reaction.

"Good, then," Xenox continued. "Let us suppose that the captain of our ship has no intention of heading to the Iranian oil terminal. Not, at least, until he makes a short rendezvous with this green light." Xenox pressed another button. "From Iraq. You are understanding this?"

"I'm beginning to," Kevin answered.

"Excellent," Xenox beamed. "But we have a slight problem, do we not? Even from here we can see that the red light will overtake the blue light before the blue light can reach the green light."

"Yes," Kevin said. "It looks fairly evident."

"Evident, indeed. Such an occurrence would be most embarrassing to everyone, governments, militias, shipping companies. Such things as illegal arms supply packages simply do not happen in our civilized world today. Who wants to deal with such a mess?"

Kevin thought momentarily of Lindsey Merric and the embassy staff in London. "Not too many people," he admitted. He visualized the faraway scene – a solitary oil freighter stolidly chugging over an empty sea, the sun high in a dense haze of humidity, a pale grey-blue sky, a listless crew sweating away the hours, an ethereal smell of diesel, a cook tossing bucketfuls of scrapings over the side, sharks rising to the surface in the turbulent wake to devour the garbage.

- - -

The captain yawned and put down his stained white mug of black coffee. He stood up from his desk chair and strode into the passageway that led to the bridge. He admired the fresh clean paint, and the steady thumping of the diesel engines was calming and reassuring. He walked the short way onto the bright bridge house. The helmsman was on duty at the wheel. They exchanged nods. He checked the maps, the compass bearings, and glanced at the radar sweep that revealed a crowded sea of green blips. He watched as the radar line swept several full circles leaving trails of vanishing lights.

One blip was moving fairly fast, from the northeast, and not far away. He went out into the hot calm air of the bridge deck and saw a faint trail of smoke, bent not by wind, but by haste. He went inside to check the radar. The ship was making an unmistakable beeline for his ship without much doubt. "Full ahead," he called in Greek.

The helmsman pushed the control lever forward. "Full ahead, sir," he answered back.

- - -

"So, what should I do?" Xenox pretended exasperation. "Allow a scandal to unfold that will embarrass us all? One that may even be traced right back to here, to me? Should I jeopardize the entire operation in favour of a small part of the whole? No!'

Kevin risked an ironic glance at Chloe which Redlinger took great satisfaction in observing.

"Call out General Stations for a Fire Drill," the captain ordered. The helmsman obeyed activating a siren. The wailing woke sleeping crew members who stumbled from their quarters to the deck dragging orange life vests. Others emptied on deck from the mess hall and break rooms. All non-essential positions were vacated as sailors lined up at their assigned emergency life boat positions. Murmurs and complaints filtered up to the bridge.

The captain scanned the horizon. The plume of smoke now revealed a vessel on the near horizon. He knew his cargo. He knew the procedure. He had met and conferred with Xenox on several occasions.

"No!" Xenox continued, theatrically pounding his fist in his hand. "That is one thing I cannot allow to happen." He leaned over to a side computer panel. "No." He flipped open an aluminum cover. "What do I do? I press another button." He pressed an appropriately red coloured button. The blue light indicating the freighter winked out on the electronic map which narrowed its view closer in on the Arabian Gulf.

"And?" Kevin asked.

"And," Xenox finished. "The problem is no longer a problem. It is sinking, as we speak, to the bottom of the sea, already assuming its new role as a future sanctuary reef for coral and endangered fish species." He laughed.

The explosion ripped upwards from the belly of the hull, hurling smoke and steel fragments high into the air. The captain shuddered, no drill this time. "Sound Abandon Ship!" he yelled. The sirens moaned the alarm adding to the growing bedlam. Boats were being lowered. Rafts were tossed overboard and inflating, bright yellow on the green waters. Men were jumping into the relative safety of the perilous sea.

At full speed ahead, the ship was plowing headlong into the arms of its liquid grave.

(79)

President John Stapleton sat at his desk in the Oval Office amidst a confused commotion. He fidgeted with a pen and flipped through a folder of papers. Lindsey Merric had been summoned, and waited impassively, but disheveled, a step behind the president. Two secret service agents paced near the doorways. A defense department representative had come up from the basement where he had been on night duty. It was a small group; the circle had been kept tight on the StresChek issue. The phone buzzed and the din hushed.

"This is the call coming in now," Lindsey said. Executive office voice recorders automatically switched on.

The president punched the speaker button. "John Stapleton," he said.

"Mr. President. Good evening," Hank Bellard answered, his voice garbled but without the sinister, gangster-like roughness commonly used to disguise callers.

An agent whispered to another, "His voice patterns are scrambled. A newer program, it sounds like."

The other nodded, "Knows his stuff, that's for sure."

"This is the President of the United States of America. What can I do for you, Mr. - ?" President Stapleton paused expectantly.

"My name is not important. It is my message that is."

"Yes, I understand," the president replied.

"Please do not mistake me for a terrorist. I am far from that. I am simply borrowing what some may consider to be terrorist tactics, using anarchy to fight anarchy, so to speak." The voice was quiet.

The president hesitated. "I am not sure I understand," he answered.

"You have met with your intelligence personnel. You know now about StresChek."

"I do."

"But you do not, cannot, know why."

"No," the president admitted. "No, I do not know why."

"Before I continue, you will hear a slight click on your speaker at irregular intervals." An electronic tick snapped softly. "That is a program which ties me into several hundred communications routes throughout the world. It would be a waste of time trying to break the logarithms that control the routing switches. I don't think even your CIA has resolved all these secretive communication dilemmas. The internet, the cloud? It's all a mystery to me where these communication signals go."

Lindsey glanced at the president and shrugged helplessly. "Whoever they are, they certainly know what they're doing."

"I ..." President Stapleton began.

Tick.

"It is a simple message," Hank Bellard's voice gently warbled.

"Yes?" Stapleton inquired expectantly.

"Climate." The word slithered eerily from the desktop speaker, floating as if carried on waves, an ethereal memo from an electronic box, hand delivered to the President of America.

(80)

"Most ingenious," Kevin stated with undisguised respect. He stared at the electronic world map focused, at the moment, on The Gulf. He gazed at the roomful of computer apparatus surrounding it. The logistics alone were fantastic. Xenox global operations instantly monitored and controlled in this one command post. Maybe there were other control sites elsewhere, he wondered to himself.

"Satellites?" he asked out loud.

"Three of my own," Xenox answered, "And two courtesy of NASA."

Kevin simply stated, "Remarkable."

"Yes, isn't it?" Redlinger, quiet until now, intruded gruffly.

A squeeze of the arm from Chloe reminded Kevin to ignore him.

- - -

The Iranian gunboat had overtaken the Greek freighter quickly and arrived on scene just as the freighter's stern slipped under the waves. Plumes of mixed water and diesel smoke spewed into the sky. Noxious steam and oil slurries bubbled to the surface. The sea shuddered with muffled explosions as salt water flooded the ship's submerged engine room. Men in life jackets paddled furiously away from suction whirlpools that clawed them back towards the sinking metal shadow. A handful of sailors who had been ill-positioned for the first explosions floated on the sheen, oblivious to all but final destiny.

The captain sat in a yellow life raft with the helmsman. He waved to the gunboat that was picking up survivors. He gave the universal signal of confounded ignorance, a shrug with hands spread helplessly out, eyes rolled to the heavens. An explosion in the hull. A fire in the engine room. These things happen. Who knows why?

- - -

"Climate?" the president blurted out nearly laughing. "Climate?! This is all about climate?! Preposterous! Impossible! That can't be!" Lindsey stood agape, but remained silent. The defense department man tried to shrink out of sight in the shadows.

The silence lingered and was finally broken by another tinny electronic tick.

"But ... how can this be? Climate? These are explosive devices we're talking about," the president answered incredulously.

"They are, most certainly," Hank answered. "And ones that should definitely not be tampered with. They are designed to detonate on removal after once being set in place, unless a coded message is sent to neutralize them."

He continued before he could be interrupted. "There's no need going over any details. We all know about climate. We are all witnessing the suffering, the disruption, the devastation. And we are all listening to the endless bickering, the power struggles, the political denials, protestors' panics. The worldwide squabbling has been going on for decades and it is at a standstill just as it was when it began, if not more so."

"Yes, but ..." Tick.

"Yes, but the time has come to take a stronger hand in the matter. If nothing is going to change, then we must change it ourselves."

"But you can't mean ..." the president stammered. "You can't seriously mean ..."

"The world has changed. You can feel it in the air. You can smell it in the earth."

"What ...?"

"Never mind, a little gibe," Hank answered. "Yes, I do mean."

"But the destruction, the people, the chaos. It would be madness," President Stapleton protested.

"Yes, it would be, wouldn't it? I'm sure it's not necessary to outline what that would mean for the United States, specifically."

The president spoke quickly. Tick. "We are aware of the situation."

"I'm sure you are. We all are, it seems," Hank's altered voice quivered like a reed instrument.

- - -

Kevin turned to Xenox. "And this computer demonstration, the lights ..."

Redlinger brusquely intruded again. "Was not exactly an academic illustration."

"You mean this ..." Kevin began in disbelief.

Xenox sighed apologetically, finishing Kevin's thought, "... actually happened. Yes, I am afraid it was necessary. It actually happened, as we are here tonight." He fiddled with some dials and a live picture replaced the electronic map. "Our resolution isn't government surveillance quality, at the moment, or even standard Google Earth." He laughed and zoomed the picture in to maximum. The plume of smoke was visible. The gunboat was just a large hazy blip. "That's about as good as we can do. My technicians are working to improve resolution, but it may take some time. There are so many other things to worry about." The map reappeared.

Xenox paced a few steps to another console and pressed a series of buttons. Countless blue lights blinked on brightly on the world's oceans. Startled, Kevin gapped at them, ticking off names in his head; Argentina, Brasil, Canada, New York, Gulf of Mexico. His eyes drifted towards Europe and the Mediterranean; South Hampton, Hamburg, Rotterdam, Marseilles, Piraeus, Istanbul, Haifa, Port Said, the Suez Canal. The Straits of Hormuz where the freighter had just been scuttled. The Indian Ocean, the Straits of Malacca, Singapore. On past Hong Kong and into the Pacific, the Panama Canal. He was astounded. There could easily be over a hundred ships represented by tiny pin pricks of blue light.

Xenox chuckled at Kevin's expression. "As you say Christopher, remarkable. I must admit so," he complimented himself.

"So complex and amazingly simple at the same time," Kevin said.

"Yes," Xenox stated philosophically. "The truth is amazingly simple."

"And amazingly effective," Redlinger added icily.

(81)

Tick. The silence seemed to echo in the Oval Office. President Stapleton stared at the telephone speaker. "We do have problems," he finally said.

"Yes," Hank's voice responded. "As you say, we have problems. And now we, or I should say, you have more problems." There was another silence. "And we are not closing in on the solutions nearly quickly enough. In fact, your prior administrations have done their utmost to backpedal on most of the advances made in the previous half century."

The president moaned audibly. "Yes, but those issues cannot be resolved overnight. We must join together to move forward …"

"Please," Hank interrupted. "Please, spare me the soap opera. This is not an election year. No one really needs the performance at this stage."

"At this stage? Is that a threat?"

"No, I apologize, not a threat, not at all. It is a promise."

The president grumbled audibly.

"If I need to threaten, then this is it: the system we have set in place can, if we decide, be set to detonate when an average temperature increase for an area rises above a certain level," Hank stated flatly.

"That means – ", President Stapleton began.

"Yes, Mr. President that certainly means," Hank agreed. "And none of us wants that. We will let that remain a future threat. Something to keep in mind as we move forward, our final option."

Roger motioned from nearby.

Hank nodded. "Now if you will please excuse me and allow me a few moments, I will get back to you soon, within the hour." Before Stapleton could answer, there was a soft tick, followed by a harsher click and the phones disconnected.

Kevin wandered an innocent step out of line. "And what is this button?" he asked, reaching out towards a centrally located metallic ochre coloured switch. Redlinger's bigger, more powerful hand violently grabbed his wrist. Kevin tensed, surprised as the stronger man slowly forced his hand back from the panelboard. The two glared red-eyed at each other as a bead of sweat trickled annoyingly down Kevin's temple.

The contest was short and one-sided. The guard, at ease until now, snapped into fighting stance with his automatic-machine pistol pointed directly at Kevin's chest. Chloe gasped. Redlinger released Kevin's wrist with a final contemptuous shove. Kevin angrily rubbed the skin and swore under his breath.

"Oh no, Christopher. We mustn't touch anything," Xenox intervened with a hint of amusement.

Roger motioned Bellard over to the closed-circuit television screen. He had zoned in on the Xenox control room from his monitor in the mansion's airfield tower. "Sorry to disturb you, but take a look at this," he said.

Kevin was rubbing his wrist and glowering at Redlinger. Xenox made a motion and the guard relaxed, lowering his weapon. Roger reached over and turned the volume up. The brief altercation was over. Xenox was talking. "Oh no, Christopher. We mustn't touch anything. These instruments are delicate and as you have witnessed, in the wrong hands, accidentally or on purpose, can be quite destructive. And if you look over here, we have another ..." Roger dimmed the volume."

He turned to Hank. "Well?"

Hank sighed and looked out the windows at the reflections of the night. "I don't like it, like this. We're moving too early."

Bellard's scheme hadn't planned for this intruder, this Kevin Varyte. It had been a meticulous foolproof setup, but somehow the whims of fate had allowed a fool to blunder in. The undercover agent's discovery of the plot had been purely coincidental. Now Hank Bellard was a pawn of his own game and he had to make a move.

"Well, never mind. This won't change anything," he said.

"The authorities, the president, they know everything," Roger reminded him. "They are setting a trap for Xenox as we speak." He pointed at Kevin's image on the monitor. "That man is a government intelligence agent. We have no choice."

"I just wanted to give them time to respond," Bellard said wearily. "A month or so leeway before a first demonstration, to see if they could avoid it, if they could show some sincere effort to alter the course that they're on, the reality that might be."

"Will be, if nothing is done," Roger reminded him.

"Yes, what will be," Bellard agreed. "Will be," he added quietly to himself.

"We have no choice," Roger kindly spoke.

"Yes, no choice." Bellard picked up the telephone and punched a reconnect button.

[82]

President Stapleton was hotly debating nonexistent options with Lindsey Merric when the phone buzzed again. He hastily pressed the answer button. "John Stapleton," he said.

"Hello, Mr. President," Hank's voice was garbled again. "It looks like matters are more serious than expected. It seems we are nearly out of time."

"Nearly out of time?" Stapleton answered indignantly. "We have just been informed of this matter. How can we be nearly out of time?"

"Inaction," Bellard replied. "Long term inaction, stymied by endless denials, corporate delays, lobbyists, you name it. You know the situation."

"For God's sake man! We're doing the most we can, given the situation. You must realize that. The world doesn't stop for us. We have to deal with the given situation. We have had our hands full; the world has had its hands full, with this climate change issue, and with this virus pandemic and social upheaval for the past several years. Not to mention we're balancing on the edge of world war, again." There was a mix of anger and pleading in the president's voice.

"That's precisely why more is necessary, the 'given situation'. The given situation hasn't changed. The wars are eternal, the virus pandemic shows us clearly that the world must slow its mad consumption of fossil resources, but at every sign of hope and improvement, with the air and water clearing, temperatures stabilizing, weather normalizing, wildlife returning, the governments push the "economy" as being more crucial than planetary survival. A cycle of slowdown, followed by a "back-to-normal" rush shows no sign of changing. So, we must encourage a change beyond back-to-normal. We want real change." Tick.

Stapleton collapsed in his chair dazed. "There's no reasoning with this madman," he groaned. "Climate change, of all things. What is this, a bad dream, nightmare? Someone wake me up, please." Lindsey avoided his gaze.

- - -

"This madman," Hank Bellard thought. He slipped into his reveries.

His plan had begun festering in his mind some ten years earlier. While incarcerated, he had deliberated about his life and experiences; his years of virtual exile from a "home country", existing in a grey international world, amongst a community that dealt regularly with large sums of suspect money, shady government contracts, dubious merchandise and commodities, and with criminally aligned middlemen. Not a rosy picture for settling down in Hometown, USA, he eventually had to admit to himself.

And all the while the world was slipping into some novel incarnation of chaos that defied logic and imagination. He could see it, others could see it, and the apparent universal lack of coherent response sent his imagination running wild. If the world was not changing direction, and nothing indicated that it would in time to avert planetary catastrophe, then maybe he could provide a push in the right direction.

The "given situation", as President Stapleton had noted, wasn't stopping. It had too much momentum and couldn't stop. The system had allotted no time for people to figure out what to do. Life, the elements, hunger, all are urgent, even death would give no quarter. The "given situation" had become a highspeed train, gone amok and rapidly running out of track. It was sucking up an irreversible whirlwind of partisan, economic and political corruption in its slipstream. Hank Bellard had surmised, "It is time to derail this train."

The strategy was simple enough; taking out transportation arteries would knock the system for a loop, for sure, he thought. Designing an innocuous looking package for explosives was fairly simple, considering he had enlisted Roger as his talented electronics expert. Coming up with a function and an excuse for such packages to be placed where necessary proved to have been just as easy. Walking over a rickety ramp in prison and seeing television news clips of collapsed bridges and reports of aging infrastructure sparked his imagination. What could be a better disguise than one that presented itself as a helpful tool, and not only helpful but vital for safety?

He loved the word "safety". It covered so much territory. It was used universally by individuals, corporations and governments alike to shield everyone's hinders in any unforeseen eventuality when something went wrong and everything hit the fan. And it was the best nomenclature for legitimately milking the government of taxpayers' money. Just mention "safety" and politicians would fall over each other to provide funding. He had used it countless times when dealing with the myriad of military-industrial complex lobbyists and international oil companies. It was a failsafe word, a contract padding word, "safety". It had never let him down.

Manufacturing and distribution would be a snap. He had rapidly set up countless businesses of convenience over the years, used them while necessary to get a job done, and just as quickly abandoned them, dispersing all traces of their existence when the jobs were complete. It was done all the time internationally, no problems, no questions asked, especially if the work aided someone's government or political campaigns.

Monitoring aging infrastructure would be an easy sell for someone with Hank Bellard's contacts and experience.

He had met Xandrieu Xenox many years ago during a shipping incident of surplus infantry arms in the eastern Mediterranean. It was a great deal, unloading weapons off the Tyre coast in south Lebanon, loading up the ship with some nice bales of premium Beqaa valley Baalbek hashish, tripping down the coast a few miles and unloading again in north Israel. It was the beginning of a great and prosperous friendship, or more accurately, business partnership. Hank had kept tabs on Xenox ever since.

As, what he gradually came to call his "StresChek" idea matured, grew and took shape in his mind, Hank's thoughts kept drifting to the Xenox corporate structure. It could be the perfect cradle for his plan. Xenox had worldwide import-export influence, offices, warehouses, contacts with city politicians and national government, and most importantly a semi-secretive satellite communications system. All of this was already in place.

Roger had been a lucky bonus. He was a naval electronics engineer, a trained genius, who had spent several seasons at McMurdo station on Ross Island in Antarctica. While on the Ice, he had fallen in with some questionable civilian contractors and developed an independent anarchist streak of his own. Upon leaving the navy, he felt his retirement plan was really inadequate for the time he had spent in service. His clumsy effort to electronically alter some banking figures and pay records backfired embarrassingly. He found himself rehabilitating in prison for a few years where he met Hank Bellard. Hank recognized his worth and took him under his wing.

Hank would now merely have to reestablish contact with Xenox and present his idea; to form a company that would provide monitoring of widespread aging infrastructure. The company would identify and prevent further deterioration of society's constructions, ones that had already been built. It would be a wildly lucrative effort. Both partners had ample capital stashed away to contribute to the enterprise. Xenox had been enthusiastically receptive to the idea, and the plan had blossomed rapidly. Xenox had also remained blissfully ignorant of Bellard's true intentions.

- - -

Another tick broke the silence. "Hello, hello," president Stapleton called on the speaker. "Are you still there?"

"Here," Bellard answered. "Yes, this madman is still here."

"Now you have to be reasonable, sir. You must be," the president said, miserably failing his attempt to project an authoritarian, in-control-of-the-situation tone.

"I wish I could be," Hank answered. "But we really are out of time. Reasonableness isn't working, hasn't been working for some time, and shows no sign of working in the near future. We have prepared a demonstration, a limited demonstration, of course, but one that should give everyone a taste of what the future may be like if the system finally overwhelms itself and starts to crash."

"You can't ..." the president began.

"Please Mr. President," Hank interrupted. "I was hoping to give you more time, but that appears impossible. Tonight, we will be testing the strength of freeway overpasses and connections of the inner ring roads of Houston, Texas, and select bridges and turnpike networks within Manhattan. Much of this infrastructure is outdated and unsound already, as you know. Perhaps not expendable, but these are a good choice for our purposes. And Mr. President, don't think that you are alone."

Click. Hank Bellard disconnected leaving the conversation and its implications dangling.

The president gave Lindsey Merric an inquiring look. "Not alone? What the hell did he mean by that?"

"I don't know," Merric answered.

(83)

A pair of gendarmes paced the river walkway along the Seine River across from Notre Dame cathedral in Paris. The fire damaged building in the midst of intricate reconstruction scaffolding cast eerie shadows in the rose-tinted mist. Dawn was barely streaking the Left Bank roof tops. They passed under Pont Notre-Dame that linked the Quai de Gesvres on the Rive Droite with the Quai de la Corse on the Île de la Cité. A delivery truck rumbled loudly overhead.

"Merde," one of the officers cursed at the noise and reached in his pocket for a packet of Gauloise cigarettes. He offered one to the other policeman and struck his lighter. In the dim glow of the flame, he noticed a blue box strapped underneath the nearest stone arch. Some kind of electronic meter was visible on its surface.

"Qu'est-ce que c'est?" he asked pointing.

"Je ne sais pas. Il y a beaucoup comme ca en la cite. Quel que chose electronique," the other answered. "C'est rein."

- - -

The eastern sky cast a pale sheened haze over a darkened London. Dawn was still beyond the horizon. A Thames River tugboat chugged its way downstream towing a barge heavily loaded with scrap metal. A mate scanned the shoreline walls and massive supports of Tower Bridge as the boats slipped past. A glint of blue reflected back from the underside near a stone buttress.

"'ello, Jack," he called. "What's that then?"

Jack looked up from the wheel. "Oh, that's one of them electronic devices they've been putting up all over. Haven't a micky's clue what it is. Nothing, I'm sure."

"Just something to spend our tax money on," the mate responded. "Bloody Liberals."

- - -

Paris, London, Hamburg, Berlin, Malmo, Rome, Moscow, Istanbul, Tel Aviv, Cairo. Singapore, Hong Kong, Tokyo, Johannesburg; Beijing, a lot of ground can be covered in half a year in cities anxious to make money. Most city governments had tumbled like dominos into the StresChek scheme. Financiers were excited. Contractors were eager. And the rest had simply fallen into place.

- - -

President Stapleton signaled Merric and the defense representative. "Get on this immediately," he growled. "Notify the emergency services, the national guard, the police, whoever is necessary, in both of these cities, pronto. If this is going down, we have to be there, now, if not sooner. Call the press secretary, the secretary of the Interior, get a lock down on media coverage. I'll be preparing a statement for the nation."

Lindsey tried to be reassuring. "We have an agent inside the organization that we think is key to this matter. We have moved forces in to surround the headquarters. When our man signals, we move in."

"Yes," replied the president. "But will it be in time?"

Lindsey and the defense man left the office with no further ado. The secret service agents stepped into the hallway to wait. President Stapleton sat alone staring at his papers.

(84)

Hank Bellard allowed several hours to pass. Dawn light had raced across the Atlantic and now lingered off the East coast of North America. "A few hours heads-up is better than nothing," he said to Roger. "They should have been able to give adequate warnings by now."

Roger nodded.

Bellard lifted the special black briefcase he had brought on the jet from California. He placed it on the counter and flipped it open. He handed two loose wires with plug ends to Roger who connected them to his electronic pad. Roger flicked a small hard polystyrene plastic switch. Mechanisms whirred in the briefcase and then, whined to a stop. A silent blinking red lighted button winked on, followed by a second. Two lights, two cities.

Roger and Hank gazed out the window. The distant lights of New York City glowed beyond the low hills and tree lines. They glanced at the television screen. The emperor Xenox seemed to be finally winding down the tour of his command center. He was once more gesturing with his arms about the wonders and intricacies of his global network.

"They will never believe that it wasn't Xenox who did this," Hank said ironically.

Roger agreed. "It is the only connection they have."

With the index and middle finger of his right hand, Hank Bellard simultaneously depressed both blinking buttons.

- - -

Explosions flared in the distance illuminating the darkness that shielded New York City from view. A cacophony of scattered ground flashes lit the night. Long moments later, a dull rumble of sound waves rattled the airport tower windows. It was the accumulated drone of scores of concentrated high-powered detonations, crumbling concrete, the twisting of steel, the collapsing of bridge structures, the shudder of life grinding to a halt. It was a horrific sound, one that the City had once become familiar with and had long since feared a recurrence of, the wailful moan of collapsing buildings. The sound would continue for a while.

(85)

In the underground command center, Xenox had been deeply involved with his engineer discussing the intricacies of a new satellite tie-in. He had apologized and shown Kevin and Chloe to a small break cubicle where they could sit comfortably and have coffee with various choices of snacks. Kevin was whittling away a few hours studying manuals and going over various Xenox Corporation documents with Chloe.

When the tremors began, he knew instantly what it had to be.

"How had it happened? How could it have happened?" he wondered. He was totally dumbfounded. There was no answer, no possible explanation. He rushed with Chloe to where Xenox stood a dozen yards away. The others around Kevin listened in awed wonder at the thunder overhead, feeling the trembling floor underfoot, and watching the vibrating walls.

"Earthquake," Xenox shouted. Chloe stifled a cry with a fearful gasp.

Kevin slipped immediately into his commando training, dropping his cover identity like the cape it was. He grabbed the distracted guard's automatic machine pistol and fired on the man instantly killing him.

Redlinger was first to recover. He dived at Kevin's ankles, sending him sprawling across the floor into a computer stack. The sudden momentum jerked the gun out of his grasp. It clattered to the floor and slid out of reach. Redlinger had his powerful hands around Kevin's throat before Kevin was able to regain his awareness. The man's iron grip squeezed relentlessly tighter. Kevin's vision blurred red. The rumbling sound of the explosions from the surface dimmed into muffled cotton as his hearing faded. "So, this is what death is like," passed through his darkening mind.

Chloe shrieked hysterically. "Stop him, Xandrieu! Stop him! He'll kill him!"

Xenox faltered in surprised wonder. "These sounds from the surface, the shaking earth, and now this!" he stammered.

He gaped at the scene before him with a wide-eyed innocent stare. It was an aboriginal gaze, wild and detached, uncomprehending, yet at the same time accepting of fate. A nocturnal hyena was ripping the throat out of a wounded antelope. The moon was full behind racing clouds. This was nature at its rawest. "So, he was a government agent after all," he murmured in disbelief. "I was so sure."

The automatic pistol lay at Chloe's feet in a pool of the dead guard's blood. She had not known this Christopher Josephs long, less than a calendar year, but it was long enough. She had made her choice when she decided to introduce him into her own world, Xenox's world. That world was shattering before her eyes.

Whoever this man was, she could not let him die now. She stooped for the gun.

"Don't worry," Xenox said stonily. "Red will finish him off."

She pushed by Xenox before he could react, swung the gun high over Redlinger, and brought the solid metal butt down heavily on his skull. The man collapsed with a grunt, unconscious and oozing fluid from a gash across the back of his head.

Xenox stumbled forward, clutching at Chloe. "What are you doing?" he shouted. "What are you doing?"

The few precious seconds that Chloe had given him were all that Kevin needed to recover his strangled senses. He staggered to his feet and pushed Xenox easily aside. He grabbed the fallen machine pistol and recklessly began firing at the closest equipment in the control center. High velocity bullets slammed into the polished metal cabinets. Smoke and electrical sparks exploded upwards in the pressurized, dust-free air. The electronic world map disintegrated into splinters of plastic and glass, shards of metal and computer processor boards, and tangles of wire. The gun emptied. Kevin tossed it into the boil.

"No! No!" Xenox cried, horrified at his fragmenting universe. He lunged for his control panel, his seat of power, his throne, as if to protect it from the chaos. It welcomed him. He tripped over a stiff leg of his dead guard. Desperately trying to regain his balance, Xenox slipped on the bloody floor, and began a slow-motion fall to his death. His arm reached out for support but only found a thick bundle of shorted, sparking wires where a cabinet once stood. The deadly electronic mesh clutched Xenox by the hand and embraced him in a high voltage dance of death.

Chloe screamed and looked away. Kevin grabbed her by the shoulders and shook her. "Is there another exit?" he cried over the spitting electrical din of destruction.

The engineer and technicians had retreated to the tunnel entrance at the first signs of trouble as was the emergency procedure for avoiding electrocution. The entrance guard had fired some bursts towards the mayhem, but upon seeing their chief die, the group retreated back through the revolving door and into the main tunnel chamber. Kevin could faintly hear the locking mechanisms of the massive vault door sealing shut after they had passed through.

"No!" Chloe hollered back. "I don't think so! I don't know!"

Kevin hauled her by the arm towards the ventilation fans.

"We can't get out through there," Chloe cried.

Kevin had earlier noted the padlocked iron grills that protected the powerful fans. He grabbed an emergency fire extinguisher from the wall and smashed the metal cylinder against one of the locks. It quickly fragmented. Kevin swung the grating open.

"The fans," Chloe gasped.

Four blades turned rapidly in the ventilation tunnel. There was just enough room to squeeze through the spaces, Kevin calculated, if the fan was stopped. Kevin turned to find something, the fire extinguisher might work, to block the fan with. It was a motion that saved his life. Redlinger had recovered and found the extinguisher first. He swung it at the back of Kevin's head, but the intended blow narrowly missed its mark. The cylinder slipped and clanged painfully across the concrete floor.

Kevin side-stepped and caught the off-balance Redlinger by the wrist. He dropped with textbook jujitsu grace onto the cement and gave him a sharp tug on the arm. The decisive move was all that was needed.

Redlinger's momentum and unstable stance hurled him towards what Kevin hoped would be the concrete wall.

Chloe's horrified scream stuck in her throat. She turned and vomited. Kevin shuddered at the dull wet thumping sound he heard from behind him. The fan groaned and ground to a halt with its smoking motor still straining to turn. It wasn't the wall that Redlinger hit.

Kevin stood and held Chloe. "Come on," he ordered. His eyes stung. He looked around. Redlinger's pistol lay on the culvert edge. He grabbed it. Thick white and black plumes of smoke were filling the auditorium from floor to ceiling. Electrical flashes were spreading rapidly towards their spot. In a matter of minutes, there would be no more haven for them.

"I can't." Chloe whimpered.

"Don't look." Kevin forced her to her knees and she wriggled through the opening between fan blades. She forced herself not to think of the sticky matter dripping from the sidings and the groaning blades. Kevin followed her and started a stooping scamper up a gradually sloped metal tunnel. Acrid smoke pursued them and engulfed them. Kevin stopped and reached inside a pocket. He looked at the tiny bleeper in his palm. He moved to toss it away, but then checked himself.

"What the hell," he said. "One last thing for God and country." He pressed a button and threw the device back down the narrow tunnel.

(86)

A convoy of troops and military trucks lined the road outside the Xenox mansion, well-hidden from the gates by a rise of ground and a line of dense trees. Dean, the intelligence recruit from the West coast sat in the passenger seat of an officer's army sedan. In the back seat, nervously huddled between two special forces soldiers, sat Ahmed and Fatima. Dean did not have the heart to leave the young Egyptian couple behind in Ventura when the StresChek trail led to the Eastern seaboard. They had a right to witness the fall of the man who had allegedly killed Ahmed's father and destroyed so many of the youngsters' dreams. Dean didn't like revenge, but he could understand and respect it.

The rumble of explosions reached the vehicle and caused it to tremble. "Steady," Dean said to the driver. "Another few minutes, if no signal, then we move in. We can't endanger our agent's life by moving too quickly. If he is alive," he added soberly.

Five dead minutes ticked by as the dull thunder continued. "We better move," a special forces man said from the backseat.

"Patience," Dean reminded him. A buzzer vibrated and a green light on a dashboard mounted receiver flashed on. "That's it, the signal!" Dean announced loudly. "Let's go. All clear to move in," he shouted. "Move in!"

The car lurched forward. The driver reached for his radio. "Condition Green, repeat Condition Green. All points move ahead immediately."

The line of trucks in front of Dean's car churned into life and growled forward. As they approached the Xenox mansion gates, a guard tried to wave them down to no avail. The convoy crashed through the gates unheedingly. The guard momentarily reacted by raising his weapon, but thought better of it and tossed it on the ground, raising his arms instead. It was a good decision; he was still alive.

On a further side of the mansion grounds, an armored car broke through the perimeter wall and was closing in on the main building complex. A few scattered gunshots could be heard coming from Xenox guards, but they were sporadic and ended quickly. News of Xenox's demise had spread rapidly; there was no more reason to put up a fight. The mansion was essentially circled. Men had retreated inside, but from there, there would be no exit. Small groups and individuals were already surrendering when Dean's vehicle drove up to the manor's entrance.

(87)

From the conning tower, Hank and Roger heard the commotion at the Xenox gates and grounds. Roger fiddled with the dials on the television monitor replacing the picture of the control room, blurred with smoke, for a clear picture of the invasion at the gates. He turned the dial again to see men surrendering on the manor house front steps. He clicked the set off.

"We had better be going, Hank," he said. "Someone may be coming to check on the airfield, or worse, someone could be flying in soon." He hit a switch and all the runway lights disappeared into darkness.

Bellard wordlessly walked to the door and down the stairs. Roger set a timer on an explosives bundle and patiently followed, trying to control his growing anxiety. The waiting room was empty. Tom, the pilot, was already sitting at his controls with engines whining, infrared goggles covering his eyes to light the night for takeoff.

The two men walked out to the waiting jet and climbed the short staircase. Roger retracted the steps and pulled the latching handle shut as the jet rapidly taxied towards the runway. No lights shone in the cabin and just a minimal glow from instruments tinted the cockpit windscreens. The plane's takeoff spotlights were darkened. With all the noise and confusion from the commotion on the ground, a camouflaged shadow exit should go unnoticed.

Tom unhesitatingly turned onto the tarmac and pushed the acceleration levers forward. The jet jerked and raced down the runway. It glided gracefully into the cool humid air and banked immediately eastwards over the Atlantic.

Bellard sat next to Julia, his secretary, lover, and companion. Roger joined them as the plane entered its tight turn. They gazed back at the scene they had just escaped. The Xenox airfield tower erupted in a ball of silent flames.

"They will search the wreckage of the control center," Roger said.

"Yes, but there will be no evidence of our existence," Hank answered.

"No," Roger agreed. "They will never believe that it wasn't Xenox who did this."

"Probably not," Hank said. "But now our friend's communications network is also destroyed."

"I know, but as we discussed, we won't need it anymore. I still have us connected through Sat-Com in McMurdo, and protected by code. Any signals we need to send anywhere in our system worldwide can be done through that route." Roger grinned. "And the best part, of course, is that the US government is funding it for us through the National Science Foundation and NASA.

Best equipment in the world and we get to use it for free."

"They will never think to search their own backyard," Hank added.

"Do you think they will heed the warning or be able to do anything about it?" Julia asked.

"I don't know," Hank confessed. "Let's hope so.

I'd hate to have to repeat more demonstrations like these two, Houston and New York."

"Well," Roger continued. As far as we know, they won't be able to dismantle anything without tripping explosions while doing it. It's been set up with that failsafe measure. Them or us, it would turn out to be the same thing. So, barring any unforeseen technical advancements the governments might make, they have to live with the present situation and the threat, for now. We have plenty of leeway for new demands. If we ever feel we have to, we can always activate our Doomsday scenario."

Hank nodded. The doomsday scenario was to connect the entire StresChek networks to temperature sensitive trip wires, trigger them with a complex code and follow up by destroying the code. Then sit back and wait as global temperatures continued to rise. It would be uncontrolled devastation. No one wanted to do that, but it was an option as long as StresChek remained operative.

Hank patted Roger on the shoulder. "Perhaps." He looked at Julia. "San Moritz?"

Julia smiled. Roger sighed and stretched. "I'll go tell Tom," he said and joined the pilot for the remainder of the trip.

[88]

Smoke billowed behind them as Kevin and Chloe staggered out into fresh air. There had been no heavy iron grill at this outer end of the air exhaust duct, just a sturdy screen that Kevin had been able to kick out and push his way through. They stumbled coughing with eyes streaming across a grassy slope and collapsed in the chill dew. Chloe passed out. Kevin looked around anxiously, tossing Redlinger's pistol into the bushes. They were outside the enclosure walls and fencing. He lifted Chloe by the arms and pulled her towards the concealment of a clump of trees a few yards away. He set Chloe in a sitting position and scouted the immediate area.

They were by a road. He rushed back to get the girl as a black shadow whined low overhead. He glanced up to see the dim outline of a small jet skim the tree tops and turn seawards.

"No lights," he noticed. "Well, someone got out," he whispered to himself. "I wonder who?"

His attention was distracted by a ground explosion not far away. A ball of flame erupted in the direction from where the jet had come. No time to lose now. He patted Chloe on the cheeks.

"Come on girl, wake up. We've got to get out of here." He dragged Chloe to her feet and hauled her off down the shadowed road. She stumbled along by his side in a comatose stupor. A mile or less, and there should be a house. And where there was a house, there would be a car. Next stop Canada, then perhaps Europe where they could disappear for good. Kevin's conscience was clear. His duty was done. As far as anyone would know, he died in the mayhem of Xenox's fireworks. The electrical fire was fierce and would have been all consuming. He may even be remembered with honour, a star at Langley, perhaps? He thought of Lindsey, and laughed. Kevin whistled softly to himself.

[89]

New York City – Devastated! Houston, Texas – Decimated! Twin City Terrorist Attacks! The banner headlines cried out from the single sheet edition of the New York Times. Few photographs were available but the front page showed one grainy shot of a fallen section of the 59th Street Bridge. A semi teetered dangerously over the black waters of the East River. The internet and cell phone networks, of course, were swamped with up-to-the-minute images and descriptive posts. OMG.

"Absolutely remarkable. The city in shambles, but the Times still goes out," President Stapleton said with pride. Now, there is a city with true indomitable American spirit." He looked at his phone screen.

"They had helicopters ferry the edition out to Newark," Lindsey explained. "They could only manage the one page."

"But what spirit," the president continued. He glanced at the paper's story again. "National guard and police keeping order. Scattered reports of looting. Fire department holding flames in check. A few large but controlled blazes at dockside facilities. Property damage inestimable at this time, but projected into the billions. Traffic halted."

He flipped the single page over, then gazed back at his handheld screen. "They're comparing this to a great earthquake."

"At least we have a tight grip on it," Lindsey said. "People are behaving quite well under the circumstances, everything considered. We just have to keep constant communication with the cities and keep people updated on all the latest developments. The risky panic period is already over with."

"Your personal messages to the two cities have had the greatest calming effect so far," Lindsey continued encouragingly. "Daily words from the President of the United States will keep stability. And we should be seeing normal traffic patterns established within a few months."

"Yes," President Stapleton agreed. "And Houston?" he asked.

(90)

"Now they have the Yanks' Cities! When will it End? Racial riots in New York City and Houston, Texas! Terrorists on the Rampage! Violence Explodes! Authorities Helpless!" The front page of London's Daily Mirror blasted the exaggerated headlines shamelessly.

"Is this all you could get?" Hank Bellard asked annoyed.

Roger grinned and flipped him a copy of the London Times.

"Funny man," Hank chided. Julia poured a cup of hot coffee and returned to the magnificent view of the Swiss Alps that lay outside Bellard's modest St. Moritz hideaway bungalow.

"New York City and Houston, Texas were struck by highly organized terrorist groups early yesterday morning ..." Hank skimmed the article for several silent minutes. "No apparent motive, authorities say." He looked up.

"They are handling it very well," he said. "Far better than I would have thought. It looks like their preparedness and learning curves have gone up over the years since 2001. Minimal rioting in both cities. Adequate communications. People are calmly waiting it out on the whole. Skeleton crews of critical personnel operating banking and businesses, extended leave for minor employees. Volunteer groups assisting police to keep neighborhoods safe. The president has declared states of emergency in each city. The National Guard directing traffic flow, alternative routes, road closures, etcetera." He tossed the paper aside.

"Well?" Roger asked.

"If nothing else, this gives the world's governments something to think about," Hank concluded. "People are showing a high level of responsibility and desire to keep rational order in the face of a man-made catastrophe. Maybe they will be able to get our world under control before natural global calamity overwhelms us. Some think it is already too late."

Julia turned from the window and smiled. "If only the world could be more like Switzerland," she said. "It's so beautiful."

(91)

A bright morning haze muffled the mournful sound of a fog horn. Dense layers of fog were lifted by the warming air and burned away with the rising sun.

Patches of blue sky appeared between the wisps of vapor.

Chloe stood by a window of a small cottage hotel. She had been only partially conscious of the journey of the previous night, day, and another night. She had been bundled into a car, and slept. She remembered a ferry boat. The sun rising. The radio blaring something about a terrorist attack in New York and somewhere in Texas. Overhead freeway signs. Rain. Climbing outside and into another car. Long empty stretches of highways. The sun setting and driving on through the night.

The once familiar man at the wheel, Christopher Josephs, was a mystery. Her beloved, but criminally inclined boss, Xandrieu Xenox had somehow died, she knew. But as to who or why, she had no answers. They had checked into this hotel sometime in the darkness, early morning or late at night, she didn't know. She had fallen gratefully asleep in a large comfortable warm bed and slept deeply. But where was she? She had no idea.

Kevin opened the door and came into the room carrying a full steaming breakfast tray. "A very good morning to you, ma'am," he said beaming.

"Who are you?" Chloe asked.

Kevin smiled. "All in good time."

www.ingramcontent.com/pod-product-compliance
Lightning Source LLC
LaVergne TN
LVHW061543070526
838199LV00077B/6884